M
Is For Monster

More Devilish Fun with C.D. Bitesky, Howie Wolfner, Elisa and Frankie Stein, and Danny Keegan
from Avon Camelot

BORN TO HOWL
THERE'S A BATWING IN MY LUNCHBOX
THE PET OF FRANKENSTEIN
Z IS FOR ZOMBIE

M
Is For Monster

Mel Gilden

Illustrated by John Pierard

A GLC BOOK

AN AVON  CAMELOT BOOK

M IS FOR MONSTER is an original publication of Avon Books. This work has never before appeared in book form.

AVON BOOKS
A division of
The Hearst Corporation
105 Madison Avenue
New York, New York 10016

Developed by Byron Preiss and Dan Weiss
Edited by Ruth Ashby
Front cover painting by Steve Fastner and John Pierard

First Camelot Printing: November 1987

CAMELOT TRADEMARK REG. U.S. PAT. OFF. AND IN OTHER COUNTRIES, MARCA REGISTRADA, HECHO EN U.S.A.

Printed in the U.S.A.

OPM 10 9 8 7 6 5 4

Chapter One

Four New Weirdos

By the time summer was over, Danny Keegan was ready to start the fifth grade. In the three months of summer vacation, he'd been involved in eighty-two baseball games, read fifteen books, seen twenty-five movies, and eaten more Popsicles than he could count. He was not bored, exactly, but he was restless.

Except for one thing, he would have been glad school was starting again. It was probably too much to ask that Stevie Brickwald had moved away during the summer.

Like all the kids at P.S. 13, Danny had been assigned his next teacher on the last day of school, before summer vacation began. This gave the kids an entire summer to anticipate, discuss, and worry about what their new teachers might be like.

Danny had heard a lot about his fifth grade teacher-to-be, Ms. Cosgrove. He had seen her many times in the school yard. She was pretty and had long blond hair. He knew kids who had been in her class, and they talked about how nice she was. He sure hoped they were right.

Danny's sister, Barbara, had a serious expression on her thin face when she looked up from her oatmeal. She said, "Tell me again about fourth grade."

Across the kitchen table Mr. Keegan, already spooning up the last of his oatmeal, said, "You let Danny eat. You'll see what fourth grade is like soon enough."

"Besides," said Danny, "I've already told you a million times."

"You can tell her again," said Mrs. Keegan as she lowered her coffee cup.

Danny said, "I don't know, Mom. The surprise is part of the fun."

"Fun!" said Barbara. "Fourth grade is serious business."

"All right," Danny said, "I'll tell you all about it. Mrs. Sears is really a dinosaur in disguise, and when you're not looking, she'll steal your lunch."

"No," shrieked Barbara, laughing as if he'd tickled her.

"And then she'll drag you away to some tar pit in California."

"Really?" Barbara said. Her eyes were wide.

"I'll drag you away to some tar pit myself if you don't finish that oatmeal," Mrs. Keegan said.

They finished breakfast. Mr. Keegan left, and Mrs. Keegan would leave soon. She and Danny stood at the open front door, looking up at the gray sky. Between them, tail wagging, nose high in the air to take in the fresh autumn smells, was Danny's beagle, Harryhausen.

Danny was wearing his new fall jacket. "Looks like rain in Cherry Blossom Lane," Mrs. Keegan said. "You'd better wear your rain hat."

"I'll just forget it," Danny said.

"You won't if you remember it," said Barbara, who already had her rain hat on. Danny compromised by

2

putting the shiny yellow rain hat in his lunch bag. He and Barbara walked out into the cool September morning. Danny blew his smoky breath into the air. "I wish I could blow smoke rings," he said.

"Me too," said Barbara, screwing up her face to try.

When they were only a few blocks from Public School 13, Danny heard faraway thunder. He searched the sky and saw nothing but gray clouds. But the thunder continued and grew louder, and he glanced over his shoulder.

"Out of my way, peasants," cried Stevie Brickwald. He was crouched low over his skateboard to cut down wind resistance as he shot between Danny and Barbara. Knocking Barbara's brown lunch bag from her hand, he laughed as he rumbled down the sidewalk.

Barbara stood in the center of the sidewalk and yelled "Creep!" at Stevie as he rode away.

"Come on," said Danny. He shivered, despite his heavy jacket. "We don't want to be late for the first day of school." He strode off in the same direction Stevie had gone.

Barbara retrieved her lunch and hurried to catch up. She said, "I thought you fifth graders were so grown up."

"Yeah, well, we haven't actually started the fifth grade yet. Besides, I think Stevie Brickwald will be a creep no matter what grade he's in."

"You're not afraid of him, are you?"

Danny didn't want to lie, but he was a year older than his sister and felt responsible for maintaining a certain heroic image in her eyes. "Well," he said as he considered the question, "that pulverizing punch of his is pretty impressing."

Barbara nodded, thinking about what getting hit by a pulverizing punch might be like.

Changing the subject, Danny asked, "Want to hear about the fourth grade again?"

"Sure. But I don't believe that part about Mrs. Sears being a dinosaur, so you can just leave that out."

Barbara listened eagerly while Danny told her about how nice Mrs. Sears was and the spelling words they had to learn and the trip to the natural history museum to see the dinosaur bones. He felt like Daniel Boone or Davy Crockett, coming back to tell his little sister what the wild frontier was like.

When they walked through the gate into the playground of Public School 13, Barbara ran off to where a crowd of her fourth grade friends were waiting. Danny had given Barbara important information that she could pass along to them. He walked around the big red brick building until he found his own friends waiting outside Ms. Cosgrove's fifth grade classroom.

Stevie was still on his skateboard, crying "Look out!" and "Here I come!" as he weaved in tight circles and figure eights around groups of squealing kids who ran to get out of his way.

Danny joined Jason Nickles and Angela Marconi, who were standing against the wall, watching Stevie and laughing. "Hi, guys," Danny said.

Jason and Angela said "Hi" back.

Danny said, "I don't know why you laugh at that Stevie Brickwald. He's a menace."

"Umm," said Angela as if Danny had said a bad word.

Danny looked at her calmly and said, "And you better not tell Stevie I said anything. If he pulverizes me, I'll know why, and I won't be your friend anymore."

"You don't have to accuse me of things, Danny. I can keep a secret."

4

Danny and Jason shared a knowing glance. Then Jason said, "Look at those new kids over there."

"Yeah," Angela said. "They look kind of weird to me. I'm surprised anybody let them come to a school with normal kids. When I get home, I'm going to tell my parents . . ."

While Angela went on, Danny looked at the new kids. He didn't have to ask which ones Jason and Angela meant, because he had never seen kids like them before.

The short boy with the slicked-back hair wore a fancy black suit with a little bow tie and a cape. When he moved, Danny could see that the cape was lined with scarlet satin. At the moment, the boy was sucking something out of a Thermos bottle with a straw. On either side of the straw were— Could they be fangs?

Not far away, two bigger kids stood stiffly against the brick wall. The boy was much taller than the girl, but she seemed to be doing most of the talking. She had a ponytail on the side of her head that stuck almost straight out, and the boy's hair was chopped in a blocky cut. His shirttail was out, and he wore the clunkiest shoes Danny had ever seen. But the oddest thing about both of them was the growths that jutted from either side of their necks. The growths looked like slim metal shafts—bolts or electrodes.

Jason said, "They look like they escaped from some old horror movie."

"I don't care what they look like," Danny said, "as long as they're nicer than Stevie." He turned to glare at Angela.

"Don't worry," she said.

Jason said, "Have some gum, Danny?"

"Hey, thanks." Jason offered Danny a pack of gum with one stick further out than the others. Danny pulled

5

on the extended stick, and a spring-loaded wire snapped down on his finger. "Yipe!" Danny cried.

Now he could see that further along the stick the wrapper ended, showing it was not really gum at all but a piece of cardboard that had a mechanism like a mouse-trap attached to it. Danny was more surprised than hurt. And when he realized what had happened, he was angry and embarrassed.

Jason chortled, and Angela ran off. As she went, she said, "You sure fell for it, Dummy Danny!"

Self-satisfied, Jason said, "Pretty good. Angela will tell everybody."

"Pretty good, all right. When Angela is done, there isn't another kid in this class who will take a stick of gum from you."

"Huh?" said Jason.

Before Danny had a chance to explain what he meant, something whizzed by him so fast it created a wind that tugged at his jacket. "Wow," Jason and Danny said together.

A kid on a skateboard was weaving among the crowd much faster than Stevie had ever gone. But none of the kids had a chance to be frightened, because before anybody knew that the new kid was coming, he was gone with a rush of wind, or had turned completely around with a high-flying wheelie and zoomed off the other way.

"That kid is good," said Marla Willaby as she clasped her hands to her heart.

"Another romance born," Danny mumbled to himself. It was said that Marla was the only girl in the fourth grade, now the fifth grade, who wore lipstick. A few teachers had sent her to the principal's office for it. But nothing had ever been proven. Marla herself said that she had rich, full lips.

6

Suddenly, Stevie Brickwald was chasing the new kid. But he would never catch up, the new kid was so fast. Stevie must have seen this himself because he shot off at an angle, aiming for where the new kid had to go next to avoid crashing headlong into a wall.

Stevie stood his ground—one foot on his board, another on the blacktop—as the new kid bore down on him. Then—Danny couldn't be sure he saw what he thought he saw—just as it seemed that the new kid was going to crash into Stevie, he leaped high over Stevie's head while his skateboard rolled between Stevie's legs. The new kid landed on his skateboard, rolled a few feet away, did a snappy racing turn, and faced Stevie.

While Stevie glared at the newcomer, Danny and the rest of his classmates couldn't help applauding. Even as he clapped, though, Jason said, "Oh no. Not another one."

Danny could see what Jason meant. This kid looked like an escapee from a horror movie too. He had a huge mane of hair that swept back from his low forehead and ears that seemed just the least little bit pointed. The smudge on the tip of his nose was exactly the same shade of gray as a dog's nose. He seemed pleased with his skateboard performance, but he often glanced worriedly at the darkening sky.

Marla Willaby said, "I don't know. I've always liked dogs, and he kind of reminds me of a puppy." She smoothed her skirt over her nonexistent hips and sashayed over to the new kid.

Stevie was already there. He said, "You think you're pretty hot on a skateboard, don't you?"

"Oh, I'm OK," the hairy new kid said.

"Leave him alone, Stevie," said Marla. To the new kid she said, "Hi. I'm Marla Willaby." She smiled brightly at him.

7

"I'm Howie Wolfner," the new kid said with an English accent. He put out his hand to shake Marla's. Looking puzzled, Marla took it and they shook.

"Wolfner?" Stevie said. "You mean like this?" Stevie threw back his head and gave a long, wolflike howl.

Danny thought Stevie's howl sounded pretty realistic until Howie said, "No. More like *this*, actually." He threw back *his* head and howled. This howl made Danny nervous and raised the tiny hairs on the back of his neck. The other kids must have felt the same way because they all got quiet and bunched up closer together. "Pretty good," said Stevie, smiling without warmth.

The silence was broken by Angela Marconi, who bustled over to the group around Howie and told them how Jason had fooled Danny with the mousetrap chewing gum. Jason and Stevie laughed as if this was the funniest thing they had ever heard. Danny didn't understand how Jason could laugh at this once, let alone twice. Howie did not laugh. He said, "Laughing at the expense of another is not the mark of a gentleman."

"Yeah, gentleman," said Marla. As she pulled Howie away from the group, she said, "I guess you're not from around here."

Jason and Stevie turned to each other, and together they said "Gentleman," and once more collapsed with laughter.

Well, Danny thought, if Jason and Stevie didn't like Howie, he was probably OK. Maybe those other monster kids were OK too. He was about to walk over and introduce himself when the school bell rang. Everybody ran up the single flight of stone steps into the building. Fifth grade was about to begin.

Chapter Two

A Miniature P.S. 13

When Danny entered the fifth grade room, Ms. Cosgrove was saying "Please find a seat. Any seat. Please take a seat." Boy, she smiles a lot, Danny thought.

When the class was settled, Ms. Cosgrove said "Good morning" and told them who she was. Danny could see by the expressions on the boys' faces that half of them were already ga-ga over Ms. Cosgrove. Danny had to admit that the big kids had been right about her. He already kind of liked her himself. He had the feeling he would probably enjoy the fifth grade.

But he'd been fooled before. A lot of teachers were nice on the first day just to suck you in. Later, they gave too much homework, or made a lot of red marks in their attendance books. You had to be careful.

Ms. Cosgrove went on to tell the class that she had been teaching fifth grade at P.S. 13 for ten years and that she looked forward to a terrific eleventh year. "We'll learn all kinds of stuff about each other and about our world." Danny had never had a teacher like Ms. Cosgrove before. She talked like one of those educational shows on public TV.

Ms. Cosgrove said, "Now I want to know about you. When it's your turn, I want each of you to stand up and tell us your name and a little about yourself."

Everybody groaned. Not even Angela Marconi, girl blabbermouth, enjoyed talking in class in front of the teacher and everybody.

Starting at one end of the room, each kid got up, said his or her name, and tried to sit down. But Ms. Cosgrove wouldn't let anybody stop there. She asked what their mothers and fathers did during the day. She asked what kind of TV and movies and books they liked. She asked about hobbies. And every time somebody said something, Ms. Cosgrove said, "Gee, that's interesting." Or, "I like that too." Or even, "I'd like to hear more about that. Maybe you could bring that in for show-and-tell." Ms. Cosgrove seemed to be enthusiastic about *everything*.

The kids fidgeted a good deal during all this. Most of them had been in class together since kindergarten. They either knew all there was to know about a kid, or they couldn't care less. But everybody sat up a little straighter and listened when the strange new kids spoke up.

Even Ms. Cosgrove spoke to them very slowly and carefully. As if she knew they were special, but didn't quite know how, so she was being very cautious. As if they were, maybe, radioactive.

First up was the kid with the fangs and the tuxedo. He said, "Allow me to introduce myself. I am C.D. Bitesky." He had kind of a funny rolling way of talking.

Stevie said, "Allow me to introduce myself," trying to copy the way C.D. spoke. Jason, sitting next to

Stevie, said, "Ok. Go ahead." The class laughed. Ms. Cosgrove frowned at Stevie and the kids stopped. Danny had never before seen a teacher who could control Stevie with such ease.

Under Ms. Cosgrove's prodding, C.D. admitted that he and his family had come from Transylvania so that his father could open his Stitch in Time Tailoring Service in Brooklyn.

"What's that you're drinking, C.D.?" said Ms. Cosgrove gently. "You know, we don't allow eating or drinking during class."

C.D. gently set down his Thermos bottle. His lips were very red. Whether this was from the stuff he'd been drinking or from something else, Danny didn't know. Maybe he had rich lips like Marla Willaby.

With a flourish and a snap of silk, C.D. wrapped his cape tightly around himself and strode to the front of the room. No one said a word, and even Ms. Cosgrove looked worried about what C.D. might do when he reached her. C.D. stared at her for a moment, and she stared back as if hypnotized. She leaned up and back a little as if she were about to lose her balance.

Then with a sudden pop, C.D. opened his cape wide like a pair of wings to show the scarlet satin. Everybody jumped. Ms. Cosgrove touched a table to catch herself. "Yes?" Ms. Cosgrove said.

Moving quickly, C.D. pulled a small scroll from a pocket. It was tied with a thin red ribbon. With a small bow, he handed the scroll to Ms. Cosgrove, folded the cape about himself again, and returned to his seat.

Ms. Cosgrove hurriedly unrolled the scroll and read what was inside. Whatever it said seemed to relieve her of some burden. She said, "We'll discuss this later, C.D. For now, you may continue to drink your, er"—she referred to the scroll—"your Fluid of Life."

Next to C.D. Bitesky was Howie Wolfner. He stood up, glanced nervously out the window at the lowering sky, and told the class that he and his family were from England. His father was in the fabric business. "And," said Howie, "the entire family is interested in astronomy. Particularly in the moon."

"Why don't you ride there on your skateboard, hot shot?"

"Stevie!" Ms. Cosgrove said.

"Sorry, Ms. Cosgrove."

"If you are really as accomplished a skateboarder as Stevie seems to think," Ms. Cosgrove said, "perhaps you could give us a demonstration sometime."

"Right-o," said Howie.

Howie sat down and dug the biggest of the new kids gently in the ribs with his elbow. "Your innings," he whispered as he looked out the window again. He seemed as interested in the weather as a farmer.

The big boy stood up and smiled shyly but said nothing. Ms. Cosgrove just stared at him for a moment. It was obvious she was just as curious about the growths on his neck as any of the kids. She blinked and shook herself and said helpfully, "Don't be nervous. Please tell us your name." She spoke carefully and distinctly, as if she thought the kid were a little slow.

"Frankie Stein," said the big boy in a voice that sounded as if he'd dredged it up from the bottom of a gravel pit.

"Won't you tell us a little about yourself?"

The girl next to Frankie stood up. "Excuse me, Ms. Cosgrove," the girl said. "I am Frankie's sister, Elisa. Frankie is not much of a talker. If it is all right with you, I will speak for both of us." Danny could tell from the way she talked that she was from some European place too.

Ms. Cosgrove nodded.

Elisa said, "We came here from West Germany with our parents. Our father, Dr. Viktor Stein, is working on a government project that is so secret he will not tell even us about it. Our mother is busy keeping our home laboratory in order."

Elisa sat down. Ms. Cosgrove said, "Is there anything else you'd like to tell us?"

Stevie punched Jason in the shoulder, and Jason said, "Yeah. Maybe she'd like to tell us how they keep their heads screwed on so tight."

Only Stevie laughed. Frankie looked pleadingly at Elisa. Elisa's expression did not change from one of polite interest.

Ms. Cosgrove said, "Stevie, I think you'd better sit someplace else." She moved him across the room from Jason. They made faces at each other, but everybody ignored them.

Elisa said, "That is fine. Everybody must be curious about these bolts in our necks."

"Well . . ." said Ms. Cosgrove.

"That is fine," Elisa said again. "They are not really bolts, of course. They are part of the neck braces that Frankie and I must wear since the terrible automobile accident."

"Thank you, Elisa," said Ms. Cosgrove. "That'll be all."

Ms. Cosgrove finished off the rest of the class. Same old boring kids, Danny thought. Stevie Brickwald had not moved away during the summer, but Ms. Cosgrove looked as if she could handle him. And those monster kids looked friendly enough. Maybe fifth grade would be OK.

After the last kid had told as much as Ms. Cosgrove could worm out of him, she said, "I know you're all eager to get started with this year's classwork, but first I want to talk about Parents' Night."

Parents' Night? Danny had been involved with such things before, and he did not like them. He could tell from the stir among the other kids that the idea of parents visiting school made all of them nervous. Parents belonged at home. When they got together with teachers, nothing but trouble could result.

To make matters worse, Danny had heard that Ms. Cosgrove always made a big deal out of Parents' Night. She was famous for it throughout the school. She had made a model of P.S. 13 that she dragged out each year and used as a kind of centerpiece for the event. Despite his feelings about Parents' Night itself, Danny was curious to see with his own eyes whether the model was as impressive as some of the big kids said it was.

Ms. Cosgrove explained that one night soon, all their parents would be invited to school. "Your parents and I can meet, and they can meet one another. We will all talk about what you will be learning this year." She looked around at her class and smiled. She really had a beautiful smile. Danny felt that even if she gave a lot of homework, he might still be in love with her. She said, "Don't all look so glum. I've done this every year for ten years, and it always works out just fine. I haven't lost a parent or a student yet."

Danny and the other kids smiled back at Ms. Cosgrove. It was difficult not to.

She picked up a big red scrapbook that had been standing on the chalk rail behind her and sat down in a kid-size chair. She might as well have been squatting.

"Gather around, everyone, I have something to show you."

With much scraping of chairs, the kids got up and stood around Ms. Cosgrove. They looked down at the book she was opening in her lap. "These," she said, "are photographs taken at past Parents' Nights." She turned the pages. Each photograph was pretty much the same. It showed Ms. Cosgrove and some kids and parents standing around the famous model.

The model was of P.S. 13, and it looked as if it were made from the same red brick and stone as the real building. It took up most of one desk top, and some of the kids in the pictures could barely see over the roof of it. Each window seemed to glow with a yellow light the same color as the real window shades. Tiny lights hanging from the top of the model spelled out WELCOME PARENTS. Outside of a department store window at Christmas time, or in a museum, Danny had never seen anything like it.

"I built this model of P.S. 13 myself from plaster and odds and ends I had in the garage," said Ms. Cosgrove.

"Imagine," said Marla.

"You don't get any older," Arthur Finster said as he studied the photographs.

Ms. Cosgrove seemed pleased by that. She said, "All right, take your seats, and I'll show you the real model. Frankie, would you please help me?"

Flushed with embarrassment, Frankie got up and lumbered to the cabinet where Ms. Cosgrove was waiting. As if she were unloading a piece of furniture from a truck, Ms. Cosgrove pulled the model off the shelf and lowered it into Frankie's waiting hands. Stiff-legged, they carried the heavy thing to Angela's desk.

The kids gathered around again. Danny could see that

Angela enjoyed being the center of attention, even if she was only basking in the glory reflected from the model.

C.D. said, "I could build a model like this showing the battered battlements of the Bitesky family castle in Transylvania."

Howie said, "It's jolly well fascinating."

For the first time, Frankie showed some life. He looked closely at the model. "Nice workmanship," he said. "But the lights are in series. If one goes out, they all will go out. I can make them in parallel for you."

"And he can, too," Elisa said proudly.

"Thank you, Frankie," said Ms. Cosgrove, "but that would probably be more trouble than it's worth. We'd have to take the entire model apart to get to the wires. What I want to know now is, do we have a volunteer who will officially welcome the parents that night?"

The kids giggled and shuffled their feet and looked at one another. Two hands went up. One belonged to C.D., and the other to Stevie Brickwald.

"Well, let's see," Ms. Cosgrove said.

Danny saw Stevie glaring at C.D. and making a fist which he hid from Ms. Cosgrove down by his side. C.D. saw the look and the fist too. He bowed and put his hand down.

"Anybody else?" said Ms. Cosgrove hopefully.

Danny didn't want to risk Stevie's famous pulverizing punch, and it looked as if none of the other students did either.

Ms. Cosgrove sighed. "Well, Stevie," she said, "I guess you are the only one brave enough to take on the parents. Thank you."

At recess time, the sky was still overcast. Danny saw C.D. walk off toward some tall evergreen trees by himself. Elisa ran off to play with the girls while the boys played kickball.

Arthur Finster chose Frankie for his team, but soon found out this was a mistake. Frankie was big, but he was not a good ball player. His kicked balls tended to be screaming fouls. His fielding was no better. Even when a ball was coming right at him, he usually shied away from it instead of attempting to catch it.

Howie was the star of the game, a circumstance that Stevie did not like. Howie was playing second base, but he kept looking back at deep center field, where Arthur had buried Frankie to keep him out of the way.

Danny watched from the bench as Stevie swaggered up to home plate. "I'm going to kick that ball to Cleveland," he said and pointed far over Frankie's head.

Arthur Finster rolled the ball to Stevie. Stevie reared back and gave the ball such a tremendous kick Danny believed it might actually fly to Cleveland. Stevie, thinking his home run was made, jogged toward first base.

Watching the ball, Howie ran back and back and back until he bumped into Frankie. In a second, he was up Frankie like a cat up a tree and, standing on Frankie's shoulders, he caught the ball. He fell backward off Frankie, did a flip, and landed on his feet, ball in hand. Then the bell to signal the end of recess rang.

"We won!" Arthur cried.

"Good show," said Howie and shook hands with Frankie.

By this time, Stevie had nearly made it to first base. When he saw what Howie had done, he stood there between home and first, clutching and unclutching his hands.

Howie ran in bouncing the ball. Danny and the other boys ran out to meet him. As Howie passed Stevie,

Stevie grabbed him and said, "I'm going to pulverize you."

All the boys got quiet. Nobody wanted to be the object of Stevie's pulverizing punch. Howie said, "Please let go." When Stevie wouldn't do it, Howie growled at him, a long, low, menacing growl.

Stevie let go instantly. Danny could understand why. The growl chilled him more than the wind did; it had the same effect on him as did the howl Howie had made that morning.

Stevie walked away with the other boys. "Coming, Danny?" Stevie asked, but he didn't wait for an answer.

Danny went to where Howie and Frankie were still standing. Howie was holding the ball under one arm. Danny said, "That Stevie Brickwald is sure a creep."

"He certainly needs to be taught a lesson in sportsmanship," Howie said. Frankie nodded.

"Come on," said Danny. "Let's collect Elisa and C.D. and go back inside."

"I do not need to be collected," said Elisa as she walked toward them. "Where's C.D.?"

Danny looked at the evergreen trees across the field. A black shape, like a broken umbrella, dropped through the branches. But before it hit the ground, it seemed to grow and change shape. In a moment, C.D. was running across the field to join them.

Walking back to class, Danny took a hard look at C.D. He said, "What were you doing up in that tree?"

"Just hanging out," C.D. said, smiling.

"No. I mean—" What did Danny mean?

"All in good time," C.D. said.

While Danny was hanging up his jacket, Stevie came into the cloakroom and backed him into a corner. Stevie said, "I've been watching you, Danny. You and that

Dracula and those other weirdos. Stay away from them or I'll pulverize you.'' He held up his fist.

Danny nodded. He didn't really want to do what Stevie ordered. Those monster kids seemed nice, much nicer than Stevie. But at the moment, agreeing seemed like the best idea. Danny didn't know what would happen the next time Stevie cornered him. Probably Danny would get pulverized.

Chapter Three

Children of the Night

Stevie didn't care one way or the other about Danny, but he obviously didn't like the monster kids, and he didn't want them to have any friends. Stevie was one mean kid.

Still, he left Danny and the monster kids alone for the rest of the day. Though Stevie glared at them from across the lunchroom during lunch, he didn't actually come over and do anything. Danny took another bite of his peanut butter sandwich. Most of the kids had sandwiches of one kind or another. But C.D. seemed to live entirely on that red stuff in his Thermos.

"Fluid of Life?" Howie said.

C.D. smiled and said, "It is an old family recipe."

"I mean, what exactly is it?"

"I will tell you if you will first tell me how it is that your howling sounds so convincingly like the music made by the Children of the Night."

"Children of the Night?" said Elisa.

"Wolves," said C.D.

"Oh," said Howie. "It runs in the family." He

looked nervously at the gray sky. It shed a funny yellow light that made the world look as if it were going to end soon.

"As I thought," C.D. said and took another sip.

"I do not care how he does it," said Frankie, "as long as it keeps Stevie Brickwald away." They all agreed.

Danny himself had many questions about his new friends. They were all nice, but none of them seemed quite normal. Jason was right about that, anyway: They all seemed as if they had escaped from one of those old black-and-white monster movies. Or were the children of something that had escaped.

C.D. had spoken of the battered battlements of his family's castle. Was it Castle Dracula? Had Elisa and Frankie been born, or had they been sewn together on an operating table from puzzle pieces of dead bodies? Did Howie already have to shave?

Danny thought it might be tactless to ask these questions directly. Yet he could not help being curious. Maybe he would find out what he wanted to know, as C.D. had said, "All in good time."

After lunch, Ms. Cosgrove taught the class arithmetic and a little about the Canadian province of Manitoba. As far as Danny was concerned, education had never gone down so smoothly. There were entire minutes when he forgot altogether about Stevie's threat to pulverize him.

The sky, which had been threatening rain all day, finally opened up during woodworking class. Each member of the class had a project he or she was sawing up and nailing together out of wooden blocks and dowels and wheels. Some were building trucks, some locomotives, some houses, some airplanes. Arthur Finster insisted on building a space shuttle.

The room was full of pounding and sawing and sanding when, suddenly, the sky boomed as if somebody were using it for a bass drum. Everybody stopped what he or she was doing. For a second, it was perfectly silent as the whole class looked toward the window. Then feathery rain began, making soft kissing noises against the ground outside. Lightning flashed, and thunder rolled into the room again. The rain fell harder.

A mournful howling rising inside the room shocked everyone. "Children of the Night," Danny whispered as the hackles on the back of his neck rose.

He noticed that Howie was crouching near his sawhorse, looking intently from side to side. His ears were longer now and even more pointed. His face was covered with hair that seemed to have spread downward from his forehead. His nose had shrunk to a black pug. Howie threw back his head, howled again, and was answered by the thunder.

"Howie?" said Ms. Cosgrove. Danny was certain that she had never had a disipline problem like this before. "It's only thunder," she said. "Nothing to be afraid of."

Howie howled and leaped over his sawhorse. His hands, which were now blunt and pawlike, were hairy too. Every kid in the room scattered while Ms. Cosgrove stood with her hands on her hips, puzzled but not angry. She said, "What *is* the matter with you, Howie?"

Howie growled and trotted around the edge of the room. He stopped occasionally to sniff a book or the world globe or a corner where there seemed to be nothing but dust. He sat down and scratched behind his shoulder with one foot.

"That's enough, Howie," said Ms. Cosgrove. "Why don't you go back to that terrific locomotive you're building?"

"I'll get him for you, Ms. Cosgrove," said Stevie.

Ms. Cosgrove told him not to, but Stevie was already closing in on Howie. "Nice doggie," Stevie said. If I were a nice doggie, Danny thought, I wouldn't believe a syllable of it.

"Stevie," Ms. Cosgrove said.

But by then it was too late. Howie had seen Stevie coming. When he growled and charged, Stevie ran screaming for help. Howie chased Stevie over chairs and tables. They knocked down sawhorses and overturned a box full of nails. Ms. Cosgrove said, "That's enough, Howie." She tried to grab him, but he was too fast.

Seeming to run up the wall, Howie leaped onto a bookcase, and from there down to where Stevie had been a second before. The airplane that Stevie had been building twisted out of the vise holding it against the sawhorse and cracked a wing when it hit the floor among the scattered nails.

Despite their fright just moments before, the class laughed and cheered while Howie and Stevie destroyed the room.

Stevie took refuge in a broom closet. Howie tried to pull the door open, but couldn't seem to make his hands work right. He sat back on his haunches and barked at the door.

Ms. Cosgrove said, "I'm afraid both of you boys have earned a red mark for today." Howie kept barking.

Just then Elisa Stein came out of the cloakroom with Frankie's lunch box. She opened the box and took out a hot dog that Frankie had been saving for an afternoon snack. She pitched it in Howie's general direction. When it landed, he stopped barking and sniffed it. Two gulps later, the hot dog was gone and Howie was looking for more. Elisa obligingly tossed him another one.

Howie gulped it down too. He trotted to a corner where he sat cross-legged, closed his eyes, and began to breathe deeply and regularly.

The thunder had stopped, but the rain fell heavily, making a loud hissing noise outside.

"Please come out of that closet," Ms. Cosgrove said.

"Is he gone?" Stevie cried through the door.

"He's sleeping," Ms. Cosgrove said.

"Are you sure?"

"I am absolutely sure," Ms. Cosgrove said.

The door cracked open, and Stevie looked out. He tried to argue with Ms. Cosgrove about the red mark. "I was just trying to help," he said.

"Chasing around the room like some kind of terrorist is not my idea of help." She turned to the rest of the class and said, "Does anybody know what happened?"

Danny decided that people see what they want to see. Ms. Cosgrove wasn't expecting Howie to be a werewolf, so she didn't think he was one, despite overwhelming evidence. Maybe she didn't watch enough old movies. Still, unless somebody thought of something quick, she was sure to catch on eventually. Was that OK with Howie? He wasn't awake to ask.

Elisa said, "I think he is allergic to thunder."

Ms. Cosgrove began, "That doesn't sound—"

Danny laughed. He felt that his face was made of plaster. Nobody would believe that laugh. But he laughed anyway. He said, "What Elisa means, Ms. Cosgrove, is that Howie gets kind of a rash brought on by his fear of thunder and lightning. It itches pretty bad."

"Poor baby," said Stevie. He had evidently recovered from his experience with Howie and was his mean old self again. "Afraid of a little storm."

"He told me so himself," Danny said.

Elisa nodded. C.D. made a small bow in his direction.

Howie spoke up from the corner, and everybody looked at him. Rapidly shrinking pools of fuzz still covered his face, but his ears had already shrunk and his nose had filled out. He looked almost normal. Or almost the way he usually looked, anyway. He said, "Uh, Danny is correct. Fear of thunder runs in the family. Terribly sorry, and all that. I've learned to live with it."

"I hope that we can learn to live with it too," said Ms. Cosgrove. "From now on, we'll have to keep a supply of hot dogs handy."

"Quite right. I will see that my father reimburses you for any monies spent on hot dogs."

"We all thank your father for that, Howie." Ms. Cosgrove spoke as she looked at the clock. "Well," she said, "it's almost three. I know that I've had enough excitement for one day. Haven't you?" She laughed.

"And don't forget," Ms. Cosgrove went on dramatically, "about the spelling bee tomorrow, to see if you, or you, or you"—she pointed at three different students—"will be the spelling champ of the entire fifth grade class. Study the spelling rules in your language book. Clean up your woodworking area and you can read quietly till the bell rings."

The kids set to work with a will. Danny heard C.D. say to Howie, "There is a bat's brow more cleaning up to do than I expected." He was chasing nails.

"Sorry about that, chap," said Howie as he picked up a sawhorse.

By the time everything was collected, cleaned, or taken away, the rain had stopped. Bright sunshine poured in through the big windows. Danny thought that maybe the world might not end after all. The class read for a few minutes, and when the bell rang, Danny actually remembered to take home his rain hat.

When he walked outside, the four monster kids were

waiting for him at the foot of the stairs. They all looked very serious. Howie said to him, "We've been talking about you, mate."

"You have?" Danny said. He wished his voice would calm down.

Howie went on. "Elisa and C.D. explained about that little fairy tale you told Ms. Cosgrove."

"They did?" Danny wondered what was coming next. Would they chain him in a dungeon? Electrocute him with huge sparks of electricity? Remove his brain? Leave him to wander in the fog they had brought over with them from the old country? Would he become one of the undead and have to wear a tuxedo for the rest of his unnatural life? Or did big, quiet Frankie just have a pulverizing punch too?

"They did." Howie enthusiastically shook his hand. "Well done. Frankly, that is very much like the story I would have told to Ms. Cosgrove myself, had I been myself, that is."

Danny smiled and shrugged modestly.

"We have been discussing many things out here on the steps," Elisa said. "We find that the four of us—C.D., Frankie, Howie, and I—have much in common."

"Many, shall we say, similar skeletons in the closet," said Howie.

"We appreciate your fast thinking—on your toes, as you Americans say," Elisa went on.

"Indeed," C.D. added. "You are very wise, Danny, for a kid who has not yet lived even one lifetime."

"I am?"

"Yes," said Elisa.

"We would like to be friends," said Frankie.

"Well, sure," said Danny. "What's the big deal?"

"I don't know about the others," said Howie, "but

I've tried being friends before. It's best to get some of these things straightened out ahead of time. To avoid nasty surprises later on.''

Danny could understand that. Some people might be upset having a werewolf, a vampire, and two Frankenstein-type monsters for friends. He saw his sister standing nearby, staring. "Hi, Barbara. How was fourth grade?''

"Fourth grade was OK. Are we going home now?'' Barbara sounded nervous.

"I guess,'' said Danny. "Uh, this is my sister, Barbara.''

The four monster kids greeted her.

"Well, I guess I'd better go,'' Danny said.

Howie picked up his skateboard and carried it under his arm. He and the three other monster kids walked with Danny and Barbara to the gate. Barbara did not say much. Danny could sense that she was unhappy about something. There would be plenty of time to talk about it on the way home.

At the gate, Danny said, "Uh-oh. Take a look at that.''

Barbara and the four monster kids followed his gaze. Standing on the corner across the street was Stevie. Stevie was watching them while he angrily punched his fist into his open palm.

"He will tenderize you,'' said C.D.

"The word is pulverize,'' said Danny. "But aside from that, you're right.''

Chapter Four

Threats and Promises

Elisa said, "We cannot let that happen to Danny."

"Absolutely not," said Howie.

C.D. grinned and showed his fangs. "A person like Stevie makes me feel very thirsty," he said. When he said "thirsty," it sounded like "tirsty."

"We will walk you home," said Frankie.

Barbara made frantic motions at Danny. When everybody looked at her she stopped and said, "Can't you take care of Stevie, Danny?"

"Maybe," said Danny. He didn't sound sure because he wasn't sure.

"Come on," said Elisa.

The group crossed the street and would have walked right past Stevie if he hadn't stepped in front of Danny. "Hey, Danny."

"Hi, Stevie."

Stevie kept punching his fist into his hand while he talked. "I told you what I'd do to you if I caught you hanging around with these creature-features."

31

Danny couldn't think of anything that would make Stevie get out of his way. He said, "We're just friends, Stevie."

"Ha. Monsters like that don't need any friends."

"Just get out of my way and I'll go home."

"Sure, Danny. After I pulverize you."

"I think," said Elisa, "there will be no pulverizing here today."

"Oh yeah? Who's going to stop me?"

Elisa said, "Come, Frankie." Frankie nodded. He and Elisa each pointed a finger at Stevie. Stevie laughed, but it was a worried laugh, and he backed off a step. "You going to tickle me out of the way?"

Neither Elisa nor Frankie said a word. Small bolts of lightning crackled out of the electrodes in their necks, down their arms, and leaped off their fingers. Lightning jumped at Stevie's chest, shoving him down next to his skateboard on the wet grass. Danny had never seen anyone look so surprised.

"You want more," said Frankie, "you follow us."

Stevie was so surprised that he didn't say anything. He just gaped at the Steins and tried to catch his breath. He did not attempt to get up as Danny and the others walked past him. Barbara hung back and moved on only after the others had walked a few yards.

"Coming, Barbara?" said Danny.

"I'll be along," she said but kept her distance from the group.

"Something wrong, Barb?"

"I'll tell you about it later."

Barbara knew the way home. She would be OK. Danny kept up with Howie and C.D. and the Steins. "That was amazing!" Danny said. Then, in a quieter tone of voice, Danny said, "That *was* amazing. Just as amazing as Howie's transformation. As amazing as the

transformation C.D. can probably make. You guys really are monsters, aren't you?''

For a long time, the only sound came from five kids shuffling through the wet fallen leaves, and from Barbara doing the same half a block behind. Elisa said, ''I think that what you call a monster is all in your head, Danny.''

''My head?''

''We are your friends,'' C.D. said. ''Does it matter where we come from or what sort of blood is in our veins?''

''I suppose it doesn't.''

''Well, then,'' said Howie, ''that's all right. You see, I told you it was important to work these things out at the beginning.''

''It's just,'' said Danny, ''that I've been watching horror movies since I was a little kid. Monsters were always the bad guys. It's tough getting used to thinking of them in another way.''

''Those movies,'' said Howie with disgust. He hopped over a puddle and kicked a tree as if it were one of *those* movies.

Elisa said, ''Try thinking of those monsters as just people with special problems—or special abilities. That will make it easier to think of us in another way.''

Danny considered what Elisa had just said. If he tried, it was easy to see her point of view.

He could think of Dracula as a man with a drinking problem. And it couldn't be fun to wear a tuxedo all the time, even when he slept. And sleeping in dirt? In a coffin? Yuck. But C.D. could see in the dark and fly.

And the guy who became the wolfman always seemed so upset the next morning about what he had done the night before. Still, Danny sometimes wondered what the world

34

smelled like to his dog, Harryhausen. If he were a wolfkid like Howie, he'd know.

And what about Frankenstein's monster? He tried to be nice, but he couldn't speak very well and he looked scary and people just wouldn't leave him alone or even try to understand. Even so, being the tallest, strongest kid in class would have its advantages. As would being able to generate electricity. Danny would never have to buy a battery for his radio again.

Being so different had to be a problem sometimes. Danny thought about the trouble they were having with Stevie Brickwald. Stevie couldn't be the only creep in the world. Danny said, "So, what about school?"

"What about it?" said C.D.

"I mean, Ms. Cosgrove thinks that Elisa and Frankie were in a terrible traffic accident. And she thinks that Howie breaks out in a rash during thunderstorms. And who knows what she thinks is in C.D.'s Fluid of Life? I'm not so sure I want to know myself. How long can this go on?"

"As long as it has to," said Frankie.

"I mean, am I the only one who knows the truth about you guys?"

"I think," said Elisa, "that you are the only one who cares enough to have noticed. Others, like Ms. Cosgrove, look but they do not see. We like it that way. We cannot help the way we are. But we do not have to make things worse by explaining too much."

C.D. intoned, "The main strength of the vampire is that no one believes in him. The same is true for the others."

"It's like a funeral home around here," said Howie. "Lighten up!" He shoved his skateboard into Danny's hands and cried, "Lead on, Macduff!" Laughing, Danny leaped onto Howie's skateboard and shot off down the block. Elisa, Frankie, Howie, and C.D. ran after him, hooting like wild animals. Barbara straggled behind.

When Danny rattled up his front walk aboard Howie's skateboard, followed by the monster kids, Mrs. Keegan came to the front door and said, "What's all the noise about?"

Barbara walked into the Keegan front yard and watched as Danny made introductions all around.

Howie insisted on shaking hands, but C.D. went him one better. He took Mrs. Keegan's hand in one of his and kissed it. Danny thought for a moment that the fangs might get in the way, but apparently they didn't. Mrs. Keegan seemed surprised but entirely delighted with all of them. She invited the monster kids in for milk and cookies.

"I think we cannot," Elisa said. "We too are expected at home."

"Also I," said C.D. "I would not want to spoil my dinner."

"Me too," said Howie.

When they were gone, Harryhausen bounded into the kitchen and began leaping on Danny and Barbara. Danny knelt and scratched Harryhausen hard behind the ears, the way he liked it, while Barbara threw her reading book on the kitchen table and flounced into a chair. She said, "Alone at last."

"What's your problem?" said Danny as he stood up.

"Stevie Brickwald is right for once. Those kids are *bizarre*."

"So what? Some of your friends are not exactly movie stars either."

"At least they don't have electricity shooting out of their fingers."

Oops, Danny thought.

Mrs. Keegan said, "Electricity?"

36

"It's a trick," said Danny. "Like when you walk across a wool carpet and then touch a metal doorknob. Static electricity. You know."

"I saw lightning," said Barbara.

"Static electricity. The weather has been so dry. And they were wearing the right kind of shoes."

"What kind of shoes?" Barbara said. "Besides, the weather isn't dry. It just rained this afternoon."

"How should I know?" Danny said with exasperation.

"Leave him alone," Mrs. Keegan said. "Maybe it *was* static electricity."

"Maybe it was," said Barbara, "but those kids are bizarre anyway. One of them even has fangs. And what about those lumps on the big kids' necks?"

Mrs. Keegan said, "Barbara, you know better than to make fun of the way people look. How they act is what matters, and every one of those kids is a charmer."

"You just liked it when the one in the fancy suit kissed your hand."

"Yes, I did. Now you'd better wash up if you want some milk and cookies." Beside her, Harryhausen's tail began to thump against the floor. "No, Harryhausen," said Mrs. Keegan, "you can't have any."

The next day, C.D. showed up at school carrying a mysterious box. The box was covered with a shiny black cloth, and it was big enough to hold a small dog, but no noise came from it. C.D. stood at the foot of the stairway, sucking on his Thermos, with the box between his feet. He wouldn't tell anybody what was inside, not even Danny or the other monster kids. His only answer to all their questions was, "It is for show-and-tell. I will say no more."

Stevie slid into the school yard on his skateboard, but he picked it up and walked with it to where the fifth

37

graders were waiting for the bell to ring. He stood by himself and would not talk to anybody. Even when his friends, like Jason Nickles, talked to him, he said something nasty to them and they went away.

It did not take long for him to notice the curious crowd standing around C.D. Despite his bad mood, he went over to take a look for himself.

"What's in the box?" Stevie said.

"It is for show-and-tell," said C.D. "I will say no more."

"But what is it?" Stevie bent to have a closer look and put out his hand to lift the cloth. Frankie slapped his hand lightly and shook his finger at him.

Elisa said, "Perhaps you do not hear so good. It is for show-and-tell."

"Why, I'll pulverize . . ." Stevie began. But he only glared at Danny and the others and rubbed his chest as if he could still feel the sizzle of electricity.

The bell rang and everybody went inside, C.D. carrying his box by its handle.

For the rest of the morning, Stevie was subdued. He did his work and kept to himself. Ms. Cosgrove complimented him on how well he was behaving. "See? Being nice isn't so difficult, is it?"

"No, Ms. Cosgrove," said Stevie. But Danny could tell that his heart wasn't in it. Stevie couldn't act that way forever. Eventually, Danny knew, Stevie would forget what the Steins had done to him, or convince himself that it had all been his imagination, or think of some way to prevent it from happening again. Stevie would cause trouble then. Danny spent a lot of time wondering whether he and the monster kids would be equal to it.

A while later, the spelling bee began. Ms. Cosgrove divided the class into two teams and lined them up on either side of the room. She started with easy words like "cat" and "dog" and "street." It wasn't until the word "restaurant" that students began dropping out.

Pretty soon there was only one speller left on each team. One was C.D. Bitesky. The other was Stevie Brickwald. They had both been spelling tough words correctly. It was impossible to guess which one of them might win. C.D. wrapped his cape about himself and smiled confidently. Stevie folded his arms and looked grim.

"Maybe it would be better if C.D. lost," Danny whispered to Frankie.

"Maybe not," said Frankie. He put his hand on Danny's shoulder.

"Stevie," said Ms. Cosgrove, "the word is 'numismatist.' "

"I don't even know what that means," cried Stevie.

"It's a person who collects coins," said Ms. Cosgrove.

Stevie thought for a few seconds and then said, "OK. 'Numismatist.' N-U-M-I-S-M-E-T-I-S-T. Numismatist."

"No, I'm sorry. That's wrong. If C.D. spells this word correctly, he will win the spelling bee."

"Oh yeah?" said Stevie, clenching his fists. He looked like his old self.

"This is a spelling bee, Stevie," said Ms. Cosgrove. "Not a boxing match. C.D., please spell 'numismatist.' "

C.D. spelled the word without hesitation.

"That's right, C.D.," said Ms. Cosgrove. She turned over the spelling book in her lap and applauded. The rest of the class joined in. Because Ms. Cosgrove was facing C.D., she did not see Stevie shaking his fist in the air. But C.D. and everybody else saw it.

"Recess is going to be terrific," Danny said morosely to Frankie.

Recess actually began just fine. A few kids came over

to C.D. to congratulate him on his spelling triumph, and Danny hoped that Stevie's fear of the Steins would last a little longer. But Danny was just eating an oatmeal cookie when Stevie stalked over to C.D. and said, "I don't like you monsters."

"This is not a surprise," said C.D.

"You jump over me, and growl at me, and electrocute me, and spell words that I've never even heard of."

Howie stood up next to C.D. and said, "Really, old chap, you brought those things on yourself. I assure you that if you would leave us alone, we would have nothing further to do with you."

"Not very friendly, are you? You monster kids are a menace."

"Oh balderdash," said Howie.

"And if fang-face here makes me look stupid again, I'm going to knock those silly pointed teeth right out of his head."

Howie growled at Stevie. The growl had the same wild, angry ability to freeze water that Danny had heard before, and considering that, Stevie stood up to it pretty well. He took a step back but retreated no further, then growled right back at Howie. Howie smiled. Which only made Stevie angrier.

Elisa and Frankie stood up on C.D.'s other side. Elisa said, "C.D. is our friend. We do not like it when he is threatened."

"Oh yeah?" said Stevie. He cried, "I can hurt him without coming near him. And if I want to, I will."

Howie reached out at Stevie, and Stevie danced away. "And I will," he said and ran up the steps into the building.

"How can he do that?" Danny said. "Hurt somebody without coming near him. Do you think he has a gun?"

40

"Tish tosh," said Howie.

"I fear," said Elisa, "that Stevie has something else in mind."

Seconds later, they heard Stevie's voice bellowing from the window. He was shouting in terror. "Help! Don't let it get me!"

Danny and the monster kids shared glances, then ran toward the building. The rest of the fifth grade was right behind them.

Chapter Five

The Empty Shelf

Even before he got there, Danny heard high-pitched squealing coming from the room. He almost ran into Howie, who had stopped in the doorway to look at what was going on inside.

"Help!" cried Stevie. "Get it away from me!"

Danny looked over Howie's shoulder as the rest of the monster kids, and the entire class, bunched up behind them. A black shape the size of a large mouse was fluttering around the room, squealing like crazy, its wings sounding like a window shade flapping. It dived at Stevie again and again. Stevie cowered under the attack, hiding under his upraised arms. "Get it offa me!"

From behind him, Danny heard Ms. Cosgrove say, "What's going on?" C.D. squeezed in next to Danny and cried "Spike!"

"Who's Spike?" Ms. Cosgrove called from the back of the crowd.

"My pet bat. I brought him for show-and-tell."

There it was, then. Stevie had tried to hurt C.D. by doing something to whatever was in the mysterious box. Only before he opened the box, Stevie hadn't known that it contained a bat. He found out the hard way.

Spike landed on Stevie's head, his wings spread wide, making the boy look as if he were wearing a strange hat. Stevie was petrified with fear. He did not move. His eyes were shut tight. "I'll never be bad again," he whimpered. "Please get it offa me."

C.D. winked at Danny as he pushed past and walked slowly toward Stevie and Spike. He crooned, "Children of the Night, what music they make. Children of the Night, what music they make." He kept saying it. Stevie still had his eyes shut and he was still not moving, but the words and sound of his master's voice seemed to relax Spike.

C.D. pulled the straw out of his Thermos. One crimson drop clung to its tip. Gently, still saying "Children of the Night, what music they make," C.D. got close enough to touch the crimson drop to Spike's nose. Spike wriggled, then hopped onto C.D.'s outstretched hand, and in an instant, he was gripping C.D.'s arm with his claws, hanging upside down with his wings wrapped around his body.

C.D. carried Spike into the cloakroom, where he kept his box, and returned without him.

Frankie said, "C.D. told you not to touch his box." Stevie was too upset to pay much attention. He vigorously scratched his head with both hands. "Bats," he muttered. "Bats."

"All right, class," said Ms. Cosgrove as she entered the room. She looked at C.D. "How did Spike get loose?" she said. That look was as close as Danny ever saw Ms. Cosgrove get to anger.

"I have only a guess," said C.D.

Howie said, "Stevie was the only one in the room when we came in."

"Is that true, Stevie?"

Stevie stopped scratching for a moment. "Well, sure," he said. "I came in to look for what I brought for show-and-tell. I opened C.D.'s box by mistake. I didn't know there was any old bat in there." He ran one hand through his hair.

"Seems like an honest mistake," Ms. Cosgrove said.

"If that bat bit me, I could end up a monster like him." Stevie pointed at C.D. with his free hand.

"I come from an old and respected family," C.D. said.

"Of course you do, C.D. And Stevie, it's not nice to call anybody a monster."

"But it's true. Look at him. Look at his friends."

"Stevie, apologize to C.D."

It took a minute, but eventually Stevie wrung an apology out of himself. C.D. accepted, bowing.

Ms. Cosgrove asked everyone to sit down so that Stevie could show them what he'd brought for show-and-tell.

The class settled, and Stevie got up in front of the room. From his pocket he took a snappy red automobile. As he explained that the car was a character on his favorite TV program, he twisted the bumpers, folded the body, pulled out the legs, and converted the car into a robot wielding some kind of ray gun.

Most of the kids had seen things like this before, so Stevie's performance didn't make much of an impression. But Frankie got up to take a look. "I am interested in mechanicals of all kinds," he said, but Stevie wouldn't let him touch the toy. "It's kind of delicate," he said. Frankie nodded and watched Stevie convert the robot back into a car. Both boys sat down.

"Now," said Ms. Cosgrove, "would you like to bring out your bat, C.D.?"

"He has gone to his rest," C.D. said. "I think it is best to leave him to it."

Ms. Cosgrove looked relieved. "Perhaps you're right," she said. "If no one else brought anything for show-and-tell, we'll get on with science."

Ms. Cosgrove had the science equipment all ready. The students worked in pairs, experimenting with an electromagnet and iron filings. One member of each team laid a sheet of white paper over an iron bar. The other member wrapped a wire around the bar and hooked it up to a tall cylindrical battery. The electricity from the battery turned the bar into a magnet. And when someone tapped the paper, the iron filings fell into a pattern showing magnetic lines of force.

"It is elementary," said Frankie to Ms. Cosgrove, "but important. I explain it to you." He was fiddling with his iron bar and accidentally snapped it in half.

"My, you're strong," Marla Willaby said. She breathed deeply and took the two pieces of the iron bar.

"Maybe you would like to explain electricity and magnetism to the class," Ms. Cosgrove said.

"No," Frankie said.

"He could," Elisa said, "but he is shy. A throwback to an early relative."

"Marla, leave Frankie alone."

"I want to be his partner."

"All right. But stop poking him in the arm."

"Explain electricity to me, Frankie," Marla said. She pulled him in the direction of her desk.

"Come along, Danny," said Elisa. "We will work together."

At the other side of the room, Danny and Elisa set up

their experiment. Danny said, "That Marla Willaby couldn't understand electricity if it sang rock and roll."

"Perhaps not. But it is nice that Frankie has a special friend."

"Temporarily, anyway. Yesterday she was special friends with Howie."

Danny wound the wire around his iron bar and put it under the paper. "OK," he said. "Hook 'er up. Hey, what are you doing?"

Elisa was hooking the wires to the electrodes in her neck. "You wait," she said.

Iron filings, standing on end like hairs, crawled across the paper to form up in long arcs around the iron bar.

"Pretty good," Danny said.

Ms. Cosgrove, who was moving around the room, giving help where it was needed, came up to Danny and Elisa. "What's pretty good?" she said. "Oh! Why, Elisa. Doesn't that hurt?"

"No, ma'am."

"I'm very proud of you," Ms. Cosgrove said. "Turning a liability like that neck brace into something useful." She tapped the paper and watched the iron filings dance. "Uh," she said, "exactly how much electricity do you carry?"

"I never measured, Ms. Cosgrove. Enough to keep me alive, I guess."

"Well, it's wonderful." She called across the room, "Howie, will you please get the compasses? They're in the top shelf in the cabinet next to the Parents' Night model."

While Howie dashed across the room and searched the cabinet, Ms. Cosgrove said, "Did you know that compasses work because the north pole of the earth is magnetic?" She went on talking while Howie passed out the compasses. His usual enthusiastic grin was gone. "What's the matter?" said Danny as he passed.

"Bit of a problem. Tell you about it later."

Howie seemed to have lost interest in science entirely. He didn't laugh when Marla Willaby tried to make an electromagnet work by hooking the wires over her ears. If there was a problem, it was more than a bit.

At lunch, Danny and the others finally heard all about it. Howie said, "The Parents' Night model is not in the cabinet."

"Where could it be?" Danny said.

"I don't know," said Howie. "But I suspect foul play."

"Foul! Like in kickball?" Frankie said.

"No. Foul. As in stolen."

Chapter Six

Two Threats and a Plan

"Who would want the Parents' Night model?" said Elisa. "It is not particularly valuable." She emphasized her point by shaking her tuna fish sandwich at Howie, who stood before the others, his hands deep in his pockets. Next to Elisa, Frankie sat on the bench, calmly and thoughtfully chewing on one of many hot dogs he pulled from his Bat Durston and the Oyster Men of Deneb lunch box.

Howie said, "Tsk, tsk. How hard we are on our Ms. Cosgrove."

"I am not hard," said Elisa. "It is a fact."

Howie admitted that she was right and concluded, "That model is of no use to anyone but Ms. Cosgrove."

C.D. let the straw drop from his mouth and said, "Perhaps Ms. Cosgrove took it."

Danny shook his head and said, "Why would Ms. Cosgrove steal her own model?" Over his knee, he was folding and unfolding a plastic bag that had once contained a salami sandwich.

From where he sat, Danny could not see Stevie Brickwald. But he watched as some skinny kid purposely sat on a bag of corn chips, then tore open the bag and poured the crumbs into his mouth. "Maybe Stevie took it," Danny said.

"It is very heavy," C.D. said.

Danny thought for a moment and said, "Maybe he had help."

"Still, you have not told me why he would do this," Elisa said.

"A random act of mischief, perhaps," said C.D.

"I do not think even Stevie makes random acts of mischief against teachers. He is a bully, but he is not a juvenile delinquent."

"This is getting us nowhere," said Howie. He took his hands from his pockets and marched up and back before the bench on which Danny and the others were sitting, all in a row.

"One thing is certain," said Frankie. "If the model is not found before Parents' Night, Ms. Cosgrove will be upset."

Danny had never heard Frankie say so much all at once. Evidently no one else had either, because they all stopped to stare at him with amazement. He blushed and tried to hide behind Elisa, which looked ridiculous, considering how much bigger than she he was.

"It couldn't hurt to ask Stevie," said Danny. "Even if he doesn't know anything, we won't be any worse off then we are now." They all agreed to that.

Elisa said, "But we must not tell Ms. Cosgrove. Why upset her? We may find the model before Parents' Night. If we do not, then we can decide differently."

"How will we stop Stevie from telling her?" said Frankie.

"I have an idea," said C.D.

"What is it?" said Howie. He smiled. "Or perhaps I can guess."

"Perhaps," said C.D., smiling back at him.

They found Stevie at the far end of the playing field, batting a tetherball around all by himself. Evidently his temper had discouraged even his friends from playing with him.

"Ganging up on me, eh?" Stevie said as he continued to sock the ball, first one way and then the other. He didn't sound concerned.

"We do not gang," said Elisa. "We have only questions."

"Keep 'em to yourself. I don't answer questions for monsters."

"Listen, old boy," Howie said, "our questions concern Ms. Cosgrove's Parents' Night model."

"What about it?"

"It is missing," said Frankie.

Stevie swung at the ball and missed. He waited until it came around again and batted it back the other way. "So?" he said.

"So," said Danny, "do you know anything about it?"

"Hey. What if I do? Who appointed you sheriff of Tombstone? And didn't I tell you not to hang around with these creeps?" He made no move to attack Danny, but he suddenly glared at him and said, "For all I know, you monsters took the thing yourself."

"I resent—" said Howie.

"Go ahead and resent, fur-eyes." Stevie chuckled at his own wit. "You guys took a mighty big interest in that model. Especially the big dumb guy with the deep-sea diver shoes."

"He is not dumb," said Elisa hotly.

"Do not allow him to change the subject," said C.D.

"The real subject," Stevie said, "is when I'm going to tell Ms. Cosgrove that you late show refugees stole her big-deal model."

"I knew it," Howie said.

"Perhaps you will not tell her," said C.D.

"Perhaps why not?" said Stevie.

"Because," said C.D., "if you do, I will have Spike play with you again."

Stevie let the tetherball swing past him. He let it swing past again. Danny could see that he was thinking, considering, figuring all the angles. But he was really afraid of Spike, and he suspected that C.D. wasn't fooling. He said, "I'll think about it. I have a game to finish. You creeps bore me. Why don't you go haunt a house?" He punched the ball, and it quickly wound the rope entirely around the pole.

The afternoon wore on. Danny had no new ideas about what could have happened to the Parents' Night model. Evidently the others didn't either. When he looked questioningly across the reading circle at Howie, Howie just shrugged. Elisa shook her head a lot. C.D. seemed entirely involved with sucking the Fluid of Life out of his Thermos.

Stevie chuckled to himself often, and when he had a chance during woodworking, he shared some joke with Jason Nickles. He even helped Angela Marconi clean up a puddle of blue paint that he'd caused her to spill when he really and truly accidentally jiggled her elbow. Stevie was very definitely lying low while he worked on some way to tell Ms. Cosgrove about the model without having to deal with Spike later.

Near the end of the day, Ms. Cosgrove surprised everybody by asking each student to make a Parents'

Night invitation to take home. Danny and the four monster kids looked at one another with mild horror. Somehow, Ms. Cosgrove's mentioning Parents' Night made them feel even stranger about not telling her the model was missing.

"Something wrong, Danny?" Ms. Cosgrove said.

Danny told her there wasn't, and felt even worse. He knew this was nothing compared to the way he would feel if Parents' Night arrived and the model didn't.

Ms. Cosgrove handed out sheets of white construction paper to which the class applied crayons.

Danny was still thinking about the missing model while he drew a picture of the scariest owl he could manage (which was not very), sitting in an old dead tree. The owl was saying "Guess who . . . who . . . who's coming to school!" Inside, Danny printed "You are!" and copied out the information about Parents' Night that Ms. Cosgrove had written on the blackboard.

As he printed the information, Danny's mind suddenly clicked. He had an idea that was so exciting he could barely wait to tell his friends. When Howie looked in his direction, Danny gave him the thumbs-up sign. Howie grinned and gave the sign right back at him.

Most of the kids just barely finished their cards before school was over. Danny was a little late meeting the monster kids. When he ran down the stairs, Barbara was already at the bottom, angry that she had to wait for him.

"Chill out, will you, Barb?" Danny said. "This'll only take a minute."

Pouting, Barbara sat down on a bench with her reading book. Danny noticed that it was, as usual, something with a horse on the cover.

"I believe Danny has some news for us," Howie said when Danny joined them next to the stairs.

"Well, yeah, I have an idea. I think we should go over to Stevie Brickwald's house and have a look around."

Elisa said, "You believe he is the one who stole the model?"

"He's the only person mean enough to do it."

"Quite," said Howie.

Danny walked over to the bench where Barbara was sitting and told her she could go on ahead. He had something he had to do.

She closed her horse book on a finger and said, "Those kids give me the Flying Wallendas."

Danny glanced back at his friends and spoke quietly to Barbara. "L don't know why. You wouldn't get the Flying Wallendas from a kid with a broken leg, or one with red hair. Think of them like that."

Barbara quickly put her placemarker into her book and stood up. She said, "Sure. And I'll think of *you* as just a normal human being too." She marched away from him across the school yard.

The Brickwald family lived only a few blocks from where the Keegan family lived. Stevie's father was a salesman who traveled, so he wasn't home much. Maybe that was why the house needed a paint job and the grass in the front yard was spiky and needed cutting. The whole place looked a little sad and lonely.

Danny and the monster kids stood a few houses down, studying it. "Is this wise?" Elisa said.

"Wise or not," Howie said, "it is something we jolly well must do. Come on." He motioned to Danny. Danny followed him up the sidewalk, feeling like a commando in some adventure movie.

C.D. leaped into the air and, with a rustle of wings,

assumed his bat form. As he screeched, he began to circle Stevie's house.

Danny and Howie crouched as they ran across the Brickwald front lawn and flattened themselves against the house.

"OK?" Danny said.

"Quite," Howie said.

They ducked down and, after wiping away a circle of dirt, they both looked in through the basement window. It was hard to see anything because the basement was dim, and there were cobwebs and more dirt on the inside.

"See anything?" Danny said.

"Nothing worth mentioning."

"What are you kids doing here?"

Danny and Howie looked up at the sudden loud voice. It belonged to a big kid, a guy who was probably at least in junior high school. He had short hair like a Marine, and muscles bulging under a T-shirt that said I EAT NAILS FOR BREAKFAST. He looked a little like Stevie, but mostly he just looked angry.

Danny and Howie stood up slowly as the kid approached. Danny was amazed at how calm he felt. He would probably have a heart attack later, he thought, if he lived through this.

The big kid said, "My brother told me about you creeps."

"We were only—" Howie began.

Stevie came around the corner at the far end of the house, saw what was going on, and said, "Give it to 'em, Percy. They're trespassing, and they're weird."

Percy stepped toward them with his fist raised when, suddenly, something small and black swooped into his face. Percy screamed and backed up, clutching at his face, though nothing was wrong with it.

Danny and Howie ran as fast as they could away from the Brickwald house. They passed the place where they had left Elisa and Frankie, and in a short time they had reached the corner of the block where the Stein kids were waiting.

"What happened?" Elisa demanded.

Danny and Howie looked back as they caught their breath. Nobody was following them. Then a screeching black shape dropped out the sky and re-formed itself into C.D., smoothing his suit and straightening his tie.

"You saved us, old boy," Howie said and clapped C.D. on the shoulder.

"It was nothing," C.D. said.

"What happened?" Elisa demanded again, this time a little more excitedly.

While they kept an eye on the Brickwald house, Danny and Howie told her what had happened. Howie concluded by saying, "Personally, I have lost interest in whether Stevie took the model. If he has it, we will not get it back."

"Right," said Danny. "Anyway, I have another idea."

His friends groaned and rolled their eyes.

"No. This is a *good* idea." He said "good" as if it were a brand name.

After a moment, Elisa said, "Proceed."

Danny said, "I don't think we have much chance of finding the old model, particularly if Stevie has it. Maybe we should build another one."

"I have many thumbs," said C.D. sadly.

"Huh?" said Danny. C.D.'s mangling of the English figure of speech confused him. Then he saw what C.D. meant, and he said, "Oh, I'm kind of a klutz myself. But maybe if we all work together . . ."

"This *is* a good idea," Elisa said. "Frankie can build

things. He has"—she searched for the phrase—"few thumbs."

Howie laughed. "I suppose if Danny and C.D. are each all thumbs, then that is just as well. He can have some of theirs."

Frankie said they could do the actual work down in his father's lab. "He won't mind. He likes to encourage me."

Elisa nodded and said, "We have much equipment."

"When we are finished, we can play in the Mad Room," said Frankie.

Danny frowned.

Elisa said, "You are thinking of those old movies again?"

"Well—"

"You are afraid, maybe, that Frankie and I will remove your brain?"

Danny was embarrassed. Earlier he had been thinking exactly that. Now he made a goofy face and twirled one finger next to his ear. He said, "What brain?"

When the laughter died down, their plan of action was settled. Everyone would bring something useful to the Steins' house on Saturday morning, and Frankie would put it all together so that it would look like Ms. Cosgrove's P.S. 13 model. Danny and C.D. arranged to meet at C.D.'s house first, so C.D.'s father could drive them over to the Steins.

Chapter Seven

Trust C.D.

That night, after dinner, Danny presented his parents with the invitation.

"Well, well, well," said his father as he handed the invitation to Danny's mother.

"You'll come, won't you?" Danny couldn't understand his own feelings. On the one hand, he was sure that mixing parents and teachers meant trouble. On the other, he would feel abandoned and embarrassed if his parents didn't go. Barbara demanded to see the invitation too, and Mrs. Keegan let her look.

Mr. and Mrs. Keegan praised Danny's artwork, though no one could explain to Barbara's satisfaction what an owl had to do with Parents' Night. Owl or not, both parents said they would be delighted to attend. Barbara made a big fuss about wanting to go to Parents' Night too.

"If they wanted you there," Danny said, "they would have called it Parents and Little Sisters Named Barbara Night. But they didn't."

"Now, Danny," said Mr. Keegan.

"You think she should go?" wailed Danny. As far as he was concerned, just having parents at school was bad enough. Having his sister—his *little* sister—mixing with his friends and his teacher would be unbearable.

"No," said Mrs. Keegan. "But there are nicer ways to tell her." Mr. and Mrs. Keegan spent a lot of time explaining how Parents' Night was just for parents, something Danny thought was pretty obvious.

Then Mr. Keegan said, "I seem to remember that the fourth grade has a Parents' Night too."

Barbara was delighted to hear this. She turned her nose up at Danny and said, "And you can't come," as if that settled the argument.

"Who'd want to?" Danny said.

There was a lot to do before Parents' Night, more than anybody else in class or even Ms. Cosgrove guessed. It was up to Danny and his friends to build a new model of P.S. 13. Danny fell asleep thinking about putting a model together using the equipment in an old monster movie.

In Danny's dream, it was a dark night. Thunder rumbled as if the boiling black clouds were big bumper cars. Lightning clawed through the hard rain. Down in the lab, his friends stood around a lump that lay under a sheet on a marble slab. Danny grabbed the big switch with one of his rubber-gloved hands and threw it. Static fizzed around big spinners and buzzed up between two wires until it broke at the top with a pop, only to start the climb again. Colored water bubbled through glass bottles the size of telephone booths.

With a loud crack, lightning struck a pole at the top of the lab and ran down a wire and under the sheet. The thing under the sheet sat up and the sheet fell away. It was a huge monster with a head like Ms. Cosgrove's

P.S. 13 model. Tiny lights went on across its face spelling WELCOME PARENTS. The words made an electric frown. "It lives!" Danny cried as his friends wildly danced around. "It lives!" He pulled off his long rubber gloves and threw them into the air.

Danny was still mumbling "It lives!" when he awoke early the next morning. He quickly dressed and ate breakfast.

Danny's parents were not rich, but the Keegan family lived in a nice house that was just a few years old. Some houses in the neighborhood were still being built. Danny had to take the bus to C.D.'s house, which was in a much older part of town.

C.D.'s neighborhood wasn't scary, but it was certainly different from what Danny was used to. The houses were much bigger than the ones in Danny's neighborhood; many of them even had huge front porches. The stores were much smaller and darker inside—more shops than stores.

Peering through the big windows of a restaurant that had only three tables in it, Danny looked at a long white counter on which he could see pans of sliced meat, olives, pickles, and many kinds of lumpy stuff he could not identify. The smell that washed over Danny when somebody opened the door was wonderful. He would have gone in and seen what he could buy with a quarter, but he had important work to do, and he didn't want to be late.

Further on was a shop window filled with piles of lace that was tea-brown with age; clocks shaped like old sailing ships; candy trays that rose in level after level like the petals of enormous metal flowers; hundreds of wristwatches, each telling a different time; glass door-knobs; and a statue of a lady who wasn't wearing much but was standing on one foot while she blew a long thin trumpet. Heaps of stuff were hidden inside the shop, in the shadows. On the walls were oval pictures of tired-eyed people wearing old-fashioned clothes.

The window of another shop held only flies that must have been dead before Danny was born.

C.D.'s house was a three-story brick job with a fire escape up the side. It was coated with many years' worth of city grime. The glass front door was clean and painted with the words FISHERMAN ARMS. In the corner of the door was a fancy arrow pointing downward, indicating the location of the Stitch in Time Tailoring Service—one flight down.

Danny went down a short flight of steps to a walkway just below street level. Over an open door was a sign that said STITCH IN TIME TAILORING SERVICE. Danny wandered in and saw shirts, pants, dresses, and coats hung on racks behind the counter. He called out, "Hello?"

A voice coming from a back room said, "Ring the bell."

"What?"

"Ring the bell," the voice said again.

Danny saw a bell on the counter. He dinged it with the palm of his hand. A second later, a tall man, hunched over as if he'd been going through doorways one size too small all his life, came out of a back room. He was wearing a long apron and half-glasses perched at the tip of his nose.

"Thank you," the man said. He had the same accent as C.D. This had to be C.D.'s father. They looked a lot alike, except this guy didn't have any fangs and he wasn't sucking on anything. Maybe adult vampires were different from kid vampires. The man went on, "I have just installed the bell. I wanted to make sure that I could hear it from the back. How may I help you?"

"I'm looking for C.D. Bitesky."

"You must be Danny. He told us to expect you. Welcome to the Bitesky home."

"Thanks."

Mr. Bitesky motioned to Danny to come around behind the counter and showed him a long, dark hallway. "The kitchen is at the end of the corridor. I believe you will find C.D. in there." Mr. Bitesky made a stiff bow, and Danny walked into the darkness.

It really was a very long hall. Every few feet a painting hung, each one illuminated by a small shaded lamp clipped to its top. Each showed a tall, distinguished man or woman wearing evening clothes. Every one of them was grim, as if he or she were bearing up as well as possible with pinching shoes.

At the end of the hall was a painting unlike the rest. This showed a once-proud castle, overgrown with vines, ruined by time and neglect. The sky threatened rain. Altogether, this was a picture to cast gloom over the brightest day.

Danny was studying the picture when a voice behind him said, "Ah yes. Castle Bitesky." Danny jumped, turned, and was relieved when he saw that the speaker was C.D.

"Is that what it is? You were right about the battered battlements. And who are all those other pictures of?"

"Relatives."

"They don't look very happy."

"As I said, they are relatives. Of me and of one another. Come. You will meet my mother."

With a swish of heavy silk, C.D. turned away, and Danny followed him into a normal if old-fashioned kitchen. Everything in it looked as if it had been purchased secondhand. Either that, or the blocky wooden table and chairs, the tiny icebox with the latch door, and the stove had been in the Bitesky family for a long time. A wide pipe led from the back of the stove up through the ceiling.

C.D.'s mother was sitting at the kitchen table reading *Hemoglobin Magazine*. She was a large woman wearing layers and layers of thin, white gauzy material that rustled when she moved. When she looked up, she smiled and said, "Welcome to the Bitesky home."

After the introductions, Danny and C.D. began their search for something, they were not sure exactly what, from which they could build a model of P.S. 13.

Danny helped C.D. move the kitchen table. C.D. pulled on a big metal doughnut and opened a trapdoor in the center of the kitchen floor. Stairs descended into the darkness. C.D. gave Danny a flashlight, took one himself, and said, "Come. We must search the catacombs."

"The what?" Danny didn't move. He had the Flying Wallendas something fierce. It was all very fine for Elisa to tell him that the monsters were just people with problems. That sounded fine back at good old P.S. 13. But here at the Bitesky home, Elisa's arguments were not so comforting. He would have to be careful or he might end up wearing tuxedos and sucking Fluid of Life just like C.D.

C.D. said, "Catacombs. Storage. What do you call the place beneath your house where you store things?"

"We call it a basement," said Danny, "but I don't know if we store the same kinds of things."

"Come. We will see." Casting the beam from his flashlight before him, C.D. walked down the stairs.

"Go ahead," Mrs. Bitesky said in a friendly manner. "I will be down soon." Somehow, Danny did not find that reassuring. Still, he nodded and followed C.D. down into the catacombs.

The stairs went down a long way. Danny kept C.D.'s heels in the tip of his flashlight beam. The air became cool and damp. Danny reached the bottom of the flight and looked around. Patches on the walls and on the thick, round columns supporting the floor above seemed to glow with their own light. Most of the sandy floor was empty, but lying there among the treelike columns were three coffins. "We don't keep coffins in the basement, that's for sure," Danny said.

"And we do not keep beds in the bedroom. Pay no attention to them. Look over here."

Sweeping the beam of his flashlight before him, Danny walked past the coffins and saw that each of them had a layer of dirt in the bottom. Either the whole Bitesky family was sloppy about brushing their feet before they went to sleep, or that was soil they had brought with them from Transylvania.

Danny found C.D. playing his flashlight beam over stuff piled against one wall. It all looked normal enough. With his light, Danny picked out wooden planks, a torn umbrella, gardening tools, broken chairs, a ladder. "Do any of these things look useful?" C.D. said.

"I don't know. Hold that flashlight steady." Danny began to move things around, hoping that some object would inspire him.

"Here you are," Mrs. Bitesky said as she approached. "That is not the place to look. Your father has some things he has been saving. You can use them."

"If you're sure he won't mind."

"I am sure. He has forgotten they are here."

As Danny and C.D. followed Mrs. Bitesky to another part of the catacombs, she talked about life in Transylvania. "Life in a castle is not as enjoyable as people who have not lived in one would have you believe."

She talked about trying for years to keep out drafts and to keep the place clean. "And on holidays, we had real problems."

"Why is that?" Danny asked.

"Imagine what family get-togethers are like when none of your relatives ever dies. Or, anyway, when they will not stay in the ground."

"Pretty horrifying," Danny said. And it was crowded, if nothing else.

C.D. said, "Mother will have her little joke."

"Is not a joke. You do not know. You did not have to clean up after them."

They stopped before a pile that looked much like the one they had just left. Danny asked a question he'd been thinking about ever since he met C.D. Now seemed to be the time to ask it. He said, "Were your family and Dracula's close?"

Mrs. Bitesky did not answer for a moment. Then she said, "Just close enough."

C.D. shook his head and said, "Poor Uncle Vlad." He began to poke through the pile.

"What exactly are we looking for, Mrs. Bitesky?"

While Danny held two flashlights, his and C.D.'s, C.D. and his mother picked up one item after another. "This!" Mrs. Bitesky said triumphantly as she flung aside a wagon wheel and pulled out a big piece of cardboard. "There should be some cans of red paint here somewhere." It was not long before she had found them too.

They carried the cardboard and paint upstairs. In the daylight that came into the kitchen through the half-windows, Danny could see that the paint was not quite the right color. "Not the same color as P.S. 13 bricks," he said.

"Perhaps no one will notice," said Mrs. Bitesky.

"Perhaps," said C.D., but he did not sound happy.

Danny thanked Mrs. Bitesky for her help. He stiffened when she smiled and bent over him, awaiting the worst. In his head, Danny had a sudden fantasy.

"Take a look at this, Dr. Van Helsing. Two little red marks in Danny Keegan's neck."

"The mark of the vampire," Van Helsing said. "I am afraid that from now on Danny will need his own coffin and a layer of Brooklyn soil to sleep in."

But Mrs. Bitesky only kissed Danny on the cheek and said, "You are a nice boy, Danny. Do not be so afraid of your friends."

"I'll do my best," Danny said as he rushed along the dark hallway after C.D., carrying cans of red paint. C.D. was standing by the sewing machine with the cardboard, talking to his father.

Mr. Bitesky said, "And my paint too! That woman would give away the store if I let her." He laughed. "That is a lot to carry. Perhaps you boys need a ride."

Before Danny could politely object, the way his mother had told him to do if somebody offered him something, C.D. said "Thank you" and bowed.

"Very well," said Mr. Bitesky. "I will bring the car around.

Danny and C.D. went outside, mounted the steps to the sidewalk in front of the Fisherman Arms, and waited for Mr. Bitesky. When the car came around the corner, Danny was surprised. It did not look like the kind of car that would be owned by people who ran a tailor shop located in a cellar.

The Bitesky car looked like some kind of limousine. It was shiny and black and had a shield painted on the door. On the shield were painted tiny pictures of bats and trees and other stuff that Danny could not make head or tail of. C.D. called it the Bitesky family crest. He and Danny loaded the cardboard and paint into the back seat of the car. There was still room for a basketball game back there.

Danny climbed into the front seat. C.D. looked in at him and his father and said, "Can you two manage by yourselves?"

"We can," said Mr. Bitesky, "but it is not polite."

"I have not yet had my exercise today. I will meet you at the Stein home."

"If it's all right with Danny."

"Sure. You a jogger?" Danny said.

"Not quite," said C.D. He looked all around and saw no one but Danny and his father. Suddenly, he leaped into the air, and just was not there anymore. Flapping before Danny's face was a big bat. The bat squeaked at Danny and flew off in the direction of the Stein house. Though Danny had witnessed the transformation before, he was so stunned that Mr. Bitesky had to remind him to close his door.

As he put the car in gear, Mr. Bitesky said, "C.D. is quite a health enthusiast. I should exercise more myself. Where exactly are we going?"

"To the top of Holler Hill Drive. Elisa said the place looks like a windmill." To Danny, his own voice sounded thick and unnatural.

While Mr. Bitesky steered the big boat of a car through the light Saturday morning traffic, Danny tried to relax by studying the interior of the car. When he inhaled, he caught the scent of age and dust. The seats were a dark purple velvet. The dashboard and steering wheel looked as if they were made from wood. "Quite a car," Danny said.

"Inherited," said Mr. Bitesky.

That sounded all right for a moment. "But," said Danny, "if nobody ever dies, how do you—"

"We have our ways."

Danny nodded. Thinking about what those ways might be, he did not say another word until they arrived at Holler Hill Drive.

Chapter Eight

One Pizza—To Go

It was a long pull to the top of Holler Hill Drive. The street wound past high walls that had thick, leafy branches reaching over their tops as if the trees inside were trying to escape. At last, one side of the street opened up into a wide lawn that rolled, terrace after terrace, to the top of the hill, where the Stein home stood.

The front of the Stein home did indeed look like a windmill. Behind the windmill part, the house sprawled across the top of the hill. More lawn rambled beyond it.

C.D. was waiting in front of the Stein house when the limousine got there. He wasn't even breathing hard from his flight as he helped Danny unload the cardboard and the paint. They both said goodbye to Mr. Bitesky as he drove away.

"I'd sure like to be able to fly," Danny said as he picked up the paint can.

"Trust me, a vampire does not always fly first class," said C.D. He followed Danny with the cardboard. Together they walked slowly along the flagstone path toward the house.

Danny said, "Whatever Dr. Stein does for a living must pay pretty well."

"He is certainly not a tailor," C.D. said.

The front door was a huge slab of wood, carved with gargoyles. The door knocker was a ring held in the fist of a metal hand. "Reminds me of Castle Bitesky," C.D. said.

Danny lifted the knocker and banged on the door, causing a loud, hollow sound that seemed to echo through the house as if it were empty. "Maybe nobody's home," said Danny. "Ever."

"We shall see."

Danny was about to knock again when the door slowly squeaked open and someone looked out at them. The door opened further, and Danny could see that behind it was Elisa. "Hello, my friends. Can you help me with this door?"

Danny and C.D. put their shoulders to the gargoyles. With the boys' help, Elisa pulled the protesting door open wide enough for the boys to enter. She welcomed them and apologized for the door. "We cannot oil it enough. It continues to squeal and give trouble."

"Get a new one," Danny said.

"Impossible," Elisa said. "My father brought this door from our ancestral home in Germany. He would not replace it even if he could."

They were standing in a round white room. A framed painting of slashes and swipes and smashes of color took up one wall. Light came from square panels around the top of the room. Elisa said, "But you are standing there with heavy things. Come with me to the laboratory." She said "la-BOR-a-tory," the way Boris Karloff used to in old horror movies. Danny's dream came back to him. He wanted to shout, "It lives! It lives!" but he restrained himself.

Carrying their paint and cardboard, Danny and C.D. followed Elisa down a white corridor. Skylights let in bright sunlight which illuminated more paintings. Some of these actually looked like something: One was of a soup can, another was of a drive-in restaurant, a third was of a girl a little older than Elisa wearing a long gray skirt that had a poodle on it. Danny wondered why anybody would want pictures like these in his house.

Danny and C.D. followed Elisa into an open elevator at the end of the hall. "Lab," Elisa said, and the elevator began to rise. Elisa went on, "Frankie and my dad built this elevator from a kit."

"Radical," said Danny with admiration.

C.D. said, "It knows your voice?"

Elisa nodded. "It knows the voices of everyone in the family. Visitors must use the buttons."

The elevator stopped with a jolt and the doors opened. Elisa led them out into a big room. After the way the downstairs was decorated, Danny was surprised at what he saw.

The place was constructed entirely from stone. Everything had wires dangling from it or spikes poking from it. Ranged along one stone wall were machines of various sizes that now and then made sparks. On another wall was a bank of bottles full of colored water through which tiny bubbles lazily rose. Each bottle was big enough to hold Mr. Bitesky. Equipment on wheels was scattered everywhere.

The big room looked like the lab in his dream, which looked like the lab in the old movies. He would not have been surprised to see hunchbacked Igor leaping around the place like a fiend.

Through a round hole in the ceiling, a shaft of sunlight fell onto the slab in the center of the room. Frankie and Howie were working on something on the slab. Howie had to stand on a piece of equipment to reach.

"We are here," Elisa called cheerily.

Without lifting their heads from their work, Frankie and Howie mumbled a greeting. Still looking around, Danny said, "Did you bring the laboratory over from Germany too?"

"Stone by stone," Elisa said. "We knew we would find nothing like it in Brooklyn."

"Probably true," Danny said. He set the paint can down next to a chair that had an iron cap attached to its back. Whoever sat in the chair under the iron cap would be held in place by arm and leg cuffs. C.D. leaned the cardboard against the paint.

"Pull up a condensifier," said Frankie, "and help us sort." Danny, Elisa, and C.D. each pulled up a blocky piece of equipment. Danny's looked like a steel box inside which thin pipes were bent up and back, making a compact bundle. The last tube was stuck into a sort of metal egg that was bolted together along its edges. A fan grew from the end opposite the tube. Danny didn't know whether this was a condensifier or not, but it looked sturdy enough to stand on.

The slab was covered with tubes, bulbs, transistors, tangles of wire, and other electronic stuff. Danny did not know the name of everything he saw. Folded on one end of the slab was a pile of fuzzy green cloth.

"We are sorting here," Frankie said. "We are looking for small wire like this"—he held up a piece of thin wire—"and tiny bulbs like this." He held up a light bulb no bigger than a housefly.

"What's the cloth for?" Danny said.

"I brought that," said Howie. "My parents are in the fabric business, you know. I thought we could use it for landscaping."

"What?" said Frankie.

"Grass and trees," said Howie.

72

They worked without speaking. The longer Danny stayed in this place, the more nervous he became. Even more nervous than he had been in the catacombs. The catacombs were basically just a basement. But the only thing this laboratory could be was a laboratory. Experiments were done here. Maybe things people were not meant to know were discovered here. Maybe Frankie and Elisa had been born—put together—in this very room! Maybe on this very table!

A bell rang and Danny jumped.

"Elevator," said Elisa and patted Danny's hand.

A man not much taller than Frankie came into the room. He had the characteristic choppy Stein haircut, and the characteristic bumps on his neck. But he wore a gray suit and tie. He wrung his hands together and said enthusiastically, "Well, my giblets, how are things going?"

Elisa said they were fine. Which is always the safest thing to tell an adult. Howie hopped off his box and shook hands with Dr. Stein. "Interesting place," he said.

"Like home," C.D. said.

"If it were only so," said Dr. Stein dreamily. "Things were different in Germany." He went on to talk about picnics in foggy graveyards at midnight. For Danny, the laboratory grew colder as Dr. Stein spoke. Dr. Stein went on, "And when it rained and thundered and lightninged"—Danny saw Howie shiver—"we raised the lightning rod and, my, the experiments we used to do." He rubbed his hands together for a moment, then suddenly stopped. "Ah," he said, "but I am not as young as I used to be."

"Beastly weather," said Howie.

"I am sure that for you, it is," Dr. Stein said. "Elisa told me about your, ah, problem."

The elevator chimed again. The moment the doors

opened, Howie and C.D. began to look sick and to scratch all over. "Something wrong?" Danny said.

"What's it to you?" Howie said angrily.

Danny drew back from Howie. It was not like Howie to take offense at a question. Normally, he tried to be the peacemaker, even when they dealt with Stevie Brickwald. Seconds later, Danny said, "I smell pizza."

"Pizza!" Howie shouted.

C.D. grabbed Howie by the arm and shouted, "What is pizza?"

A woman walked into the room carrying a flat white box. She wore a long gray gown, and her frizzy hair was piled high atop her head. A tiny diamond—it could have been glass as far as Danny knew—studded each of the bumps in her neck. The woman said, "Poor deprived child. This is pizza." She set the box down on the slab and opened the top to show them what was inside. The smell of tomato sauce and cheese was stronger than ever. It made Danny hungry.

As one, Howie and C.D. cried, "Aaiiee!" C.D. threw his cape up over his face and leaped backward off his condensifier. Howie crouched, already beginning to grow hair on his face. Screeching in distress, C.D. leaped into the air and instantly became a bat. He fluttered up through the hole in the ceiling and was gone. Howie howled and ran from the room on all fours. He did not bother with the elevator, but pushed through a door marked EXIT and down the emergency stairs.

Howie's howl had caused Danny to lose his appetite. Frankie and Dr. Stein and the woman looked around, bewildered. The woman seemed to be particularly upset because she thought that she was the cause of the trouble. "What did I do?" she asked. "I was sure the children would like a nice snack."

Only Elisa seemed to know what was going on. She

said, "Do not worry. They will be back. I suggest that we eat the pizza so that they can return more quickly. They will not be wanting any."

"I do not understand," said Frankie, "but eating pizza is never a problem."

Chapter Nine

The Mad Room

Thinking that Howie and C.D. knew something that he didn't know, Danny looked at the pizza with suspicion. He said, "What exactly is wrong with this pizza?"

"Nothing is wrong with it," said Elisa. "It is only that the sauce contains garlic."

"I love garlic," Frankie said as he tore into another wedge.

"I remember now," said Danny, brightening some. "In all those monster movies, the people use garlic to keep the werewolves and vampires away." Danny did not go on to comment that the garlic never bothered Dr. Frankenstein's creations.

"I never expected to encounter such things in Brooklyn," the woman said.

"Brooklyn's not the place it was," said Danny, thinking about all the strange things he had seen and heard since school had started.

"In the old country," Dr. Stein said, "we knew better than to serve Italian food to some of our friends."

The woman said, "Now that the excitement is over, I would like to introduce myself. I am Mrs. Stein."

"My bride," Dr. Stein said with pride.

Danny waved to Mrs. Stein, the bride of Dr. Stein.

Frankie, Elisa, and Danny continued to eat while Dr. and Mrs. Stein went back down in the elevator. "To watch for Howie and C.D.," said Mrs. Stein. "I must apologize."

The pizza was extra large, and there were only three kids eating it when it had been meant for five. When even Frankie could eat no more, there were still a few pieces left. "I will put them away for later," said Elisa.

"A good idea," said Frankie. "We wanted to show Danny the Mad Room anyway."

"Mad Room?" Danny said.

Elisa shook her head and laughed. She said, "You survived the laboratory. You will survive the Mad Room also."

Danny followed Elisa and Frankie to the far side of the laboratory, where they descended a wide flight of stairs that curved to the level below.

At the bottom of the stairs was a room that looked like an electronics warehouse. Table after table held computer terminals. Along one wall was a line of video games. One corner of the bright room had been set up like a den, with a thick carpet on the floor and big leather furniture. The furniture faced a wide-screen TV, speakers that Danny could have hid inside, and banks and banks of audio and video equipment. There were switches and dials and buttons everywhere.

"This is terrific," said Danny. "I want to play with everything."

"This is possible," said Frankie. "But perhaps some other time. We have a project."

So much had happened since he'd left the house that

morning, Danny had almost forgotten that he was at the Stein house to build a model of P.S. 13 for Ms. Cosgrove.

Elisa put the leftover pizza into a big double-door refrigerator that was standing next to a video game called Mummy Mania. She handed around cans of root beer to wash the pizza down. While they were drinking, she said, "Perhaps Frankie could program one of these computers to help us build a model of P.S. 13."

"Can he?" Danny said.

"Of course," said Frankie. He wandered off mumbling and sat down at one of the terminals. He thought a moment and began to type lightly on the machine's keys.

"He is very good at this," said Elisa. She and Danny sipped root beer while watching Frankie type a long column of letters and numbers that meant nothing, at least to Danny.

At last Frankie said, "I finish. Now, we tell the Rotwang Mark III what materials we have and what we want to build. It will tell us what to do."

On their fingers, Elisa and Danny ticked off the bits and pieces they had collected. Frankie typed in the red paint and the cardboard and the green fabric and the electrical parts.

"Not much of a list," said Danny.

"No matter," said Frankie. "The Rotwang Mark III is very smart. We must tell it now what we want to build."

Describing P.S. 13 was more difficult than reeling off a list of parts. Still, with Elisa's and Danny's help, Frankie told the Rotwang Mark III that the school was a two-story brick building with a flight of cement steps at each corner. Strung across the top in lights would be the words WELCOME PARENTS.

"That's all I can remember," said Danny.

"Me too," said Elisa.

"Very well," said Frankie. He pushed another key on the computer. The screen, on which Frankie had typed everything they could remember about P.S. 13, went blank for a second, to be replaced by the single word WORKING.

A door across the room opened to admit C.D. and Howie, now both back in their human forms. They swung their arms and tried to look casual, but Danny could tell they were both embarrassed.

"Sorry about that," Howie said. "I guess you know what happened."

"Garlic," said Danny.

Howie and C.D. shuddered. Howie said, "Fear of it is in the blood."

At the word "blood," C.D. shot Howie an angry look and said, "He is correct. We were not just crying wolf."

Howie shot C.D. an angry look. They could not hold their angry looks for long before they both laughed.

Elisa said, "My mother is very sorry. It will not happen again."

Frankie said, "The Steins do not worry about garlic. Our ancestors worried about angry villagers carrying pitchforks and torches."

Danny was about to tell them that he'd never seen a pitchfork in Brooklyn when the computer screen came alive again. The computer was quickly drawing a picture of P.S. 13 as described by Frankie, Elisa, and Danny. As they watched, the three explained to Howie and C.D. what the computer was doing.

"Frankie, you are a wonder and a half," said Howie, and C.D. agreed.

When the computer was done with the drawing, everyone studied the screen. "Looks OK to me," Danny said.

"The spitting image," said Howie.

"OK," said Frankie, and he pushed another key. At one side of the room, a machine began to chatter. "We make a hard copy," said Frankie. "In the lab we will follow the computer's instructions and put the model together."

When the printer stopped chattering, Frankie tore off the printed page, and everybody crowded around to look. "Looks simple enough," said Howie.

They walked back up the stairs to the laboratory, where they put the model together on the slab. Frankie did most of the actual work, but Elisa, Howie, C.D., and Danny had suggestions to make. The further along they went, the less the model looked to Danny like P.S. 13 or any other school he had ever seen. Unless it was an Eskimo school. The thing looked like a red (not quite the right color) igloo.

By the time they were done, it was obvious to everyone that the thing looked nothing like Ms. Cosgrove's P.S. 13 model.

"What went wrong?" Howie said.

"I guess," said Elisa, "our data was a little optimistic."

"What will we do now?" said C.D.

No one said a word. They just stared glumly at the red igloo that was supposed to be P.S. 13. Danny said, "I have another idea."

"Better than this one?" said C.D.

"I hope so," said Danny. "And it'll take all of us to make it work."

Chapter Ten

A Fairly Freaky Parents' Night

The following week was a long one for Danny and the other kids. Parents' Night stood at the end of it like a big surprise package. No one knew what was in the package. No one even knew if what the package contained was good or not.

Class time on Friday was a rowdy affair. Everybody made jokes and mistakes they would not ordinarily have made. Stevie walked up to anybody who was standing still and practiced his welcoming speech on him or her. When the bell finally rang, signaling the end of the day, Ms. Cosgrove sent everybody home with the words, "And don't come back till seven-thirty." She shook her finger at them and laughed.

Danny tried to keep his stomach in place as he ate dinner that night. At least he didn't have to say anything. Barbara monopolized the conversation, talking about all the shows she would watch on TV that night. Bowls of popcorn and a blanket that Mom would wrap around her were already on the couch in the living room.

When dinner was over, Danny left his mom and dad washing the dishes. "See you later," he said. "Don't forget. Seven-thirty."

"We can't forget," said Mrs. Keegan. "I've engraved it on your father's forehead." Mom's little joke.

Danny ran to school, wishing he could fly the way C.D. could. He was out of breath by the time he got there, and had to walk slowly across the school yard to get it back. Four mysterious shapes waited for him at the foot of the cement stairway. "Is that you guys?" Danny said softly.

"It is us," said Elisa. As if on a signal, the school yard lights went on. It was his friends, all right. Frankie had a string of red and green lights wrapped around his waist.

Danny and the others went up the stairs and into the building, intending to wait for Ms. Cosgrove outside the classroom door. But when they got there, the door wasn't locked.

"Very interesting," Frankie said.

"Perhaps Ms. Cosgrove forgot to lock the door when she left earlier today," C.D. said.

Whatever had happened, they agreed that it would be all right to wait for Ms. Cosgrove inside. They went into the room and turned on the lights. What they saw then made them stop suddenly, their eyes wide with horror. The P.S. 13 model was back.

It sat on a desk at the front of the room. But that wasn't the horrible part. The horrible part was what had happened to the model. Its top was all bashed in, chicken wire was showing through the walls, wires were ripped into wild brushes.

The kids still had not moved, had barely breathed, when Danny heard a voice behind them.

"Well, we are all a little early, I see."

They turned and saw Ms. Cosgrove standing in the doorway, smiling. She had on more makeup than she usually wore. Then she stepped further into the room and saw the model. The smile went away. Her lower lip began to tremble as she took another step forward.

"Why?" she said, her voice feather-soft and shaking.

"We didn't do it, Ms. Cosgrove," Danny said. "We just got here ourselves."

"You kids—" Ms. Cosgrove began. Even now, she did not sound angry. Just terribly, terribly tired and disappointed. She sat down near the model and laid a hand against one busted wall while she tried to get used to the idea that somebody had destroyed her Parents' Night model.

When Elisa walked over to study the model closely, Ms. Cosgrove looked up and shook her head.

As if matters were not bad enough, Stevie Brickwald came in then. He was dressed in a suit. It did not take him long to see what was going on. Disgusted, he said, "I knew you monsters would start acting like monsters sooner or later."

Stevie went over to look at the model. He pushed Elisa aside. "Have a look at this, Ms. Cosgrove. Fluid of Life! Dog hair! Those weirdos must have done it."

"It would seem so, Stevie." Ms. Cosgrove looked at Elisa, but she was speaking to them all. She said, "Tomorrow we will all go to see the principal together and figure out what should be done."

"If you please, Ms. Cosgrove," Elisa said.

Everyone looked at her.

Elisa went on. "There are many clues here that might lead to the actual guilty party."

"Please, Elisa," Ms. Cosgrove said as she touched her hand to her forehead. "Don't make this worse than it already is."

Elisa said, "But Ms. Cosgrove, this red stuff is not C.D.'s Fluid of Life. And this hair does not belong to Howie."

"Really?" Ms. Cosgrove stood up to look at the spot where Elisa was pointing. She touched the spot of red, brought some of it to her nose, and sniffed it. "It's paint," she said, sounding surprised.

"Indeed," said Elisa. "Now see if the hair matches any of Howie's."

Carefully, Ms. Cosgrove picked up a little bundle of hairs that had been stuck in the red paint. She asked Howie to join her by the model, and he did. She held the hair up against the hair on his head and on his arms. Howie stood very still, watching Ms. Cosgrove's movements with only his eyes.

"Elisa's right," Danny said. "It doesn't match anywhere."

Ms. Cosgrove said, "Then who did this?"

"Excuse me," C.D. said, "but we have a suspect in mind."

They turned and saw that Stevie was edging toward the door. "Got to go," he said brightly. "Lot of chairs to set up."

"Come here, Stevie," Ms. Cosgrove said firmly.

Hands in his pockets, Stevie shuffled to where Ms. Cosgrove and the others stood. "Let me see your hands."

Stevie pulled his hands from his pockets and held them out for inspection. There were blotches of what seemed to be red paint on his hands. Ms. Cosgrove held up the hairs. As far as Danny could tell, they matched the hair on Stevie's head perfectly.

Evidently Ms. Cosgrove thought so too, because she said, "Would you care to tell me what all this is about?"

Stevie tried to smile. The effect was neither convincing nor pleasant. He told his story. It wasn't nice, but

Danny suspected it was the truth. There's no point lying when you're caught red-handed.

Stevie had arrived early to practice his welcoming speech, and he had been surprised to see the model was back.

"Back?" said Ms. Cosgrove.

"Yeah. Danny and the others told me it was missing, so I was surprised to see it."

"Go on, Stevie," said Ms. Cosgrove. "I see that you are not the only one who will have to explain something this evening."

"No, Ms. Cosgrove," Stevie went on. He'd come to school and was surprised to see the model. That was when he got his big idea. He would destroy it and blame it on the monster kids. He dribbled a little red paint on the white parts to make it look as if C.D. had been there with his red Fluid of Life. Then he pulled some hair out of his own head and stuck it into the paint to make it look as if Howie had been there.

Ms. Cosgrove sat down. Her lower lip was trembling. She didn't know what to say. Nobody said anything. Never before had Danny seen a teacher so crushed. Then she took a shaky deep breath and said, "Steven, you are a great disappointment to me. You have not only disgraced yourself, you have ruined Parents' Night for everybody."

"And," said Elisa, "if Angela Marconi hears about this, it'll be all over the school."

Stevie couldn't feel any worse. He just nodded.

Danny said, "Ms. Cosgrove, maybe Parents' Night isn't ruined."

Ms. Cosgrove smiled thinly.

"No, really," Danny said. "We thought someone had stolen the model, so we arranged something we hope will be just as good."

"Perhaps, Danny, you would care to explain exactly why you and your friends thought the model was stolen."

"Yes, Ms. Cosgrove. Howie—"

Howie interrupted. "You remember the day we studied electromagnetism? You sent me to look for the compasses? Well, when I looked for them, I saw that the model was gone. I just assumed"—he shrugged—"that someone had stolen it."

"No, Howie," Ms. Cosgrove said. "It wasn't stolen. When I tried it out, the lights wouldn't come on, so I took the model home to rewire it as Frankie suggested."

"I was right," C.D. said. "Ms. Cosgrove did take it herself."

"Now it is gone for good," Elisa said. "But we have a plan."

"Right," said Danny. "All you have to do is greet the parents outside instead of inside, and get the custodian to let us onto the roof."

At first Ms. Cosgrove was too whipped to try anything. But Danny and his friends pleaded with her, and at last she gave in. She really *did* want to have Parents' Night.

Seven-thirty came. From the roof, Danny, Elisa, Frankie, and Howie could see the crowd of parents and their children standing in front of the cement stairway. They were bundled up, wondering when they could go inside. The kids on the roof could also see Stevie glaring at C.D. as C.D. stood on a step and spoke into a microphone, welcoming the parents.

At last, C.D. said, "And so, we welcome you to this year's P.S. 13 Fifth Grade Parents' Night."

As the parents and students began to applaud, Danny said, "That's our cue." He and Howie each held an end of Frankie's string of red and green lights. They dangled

the string over the side of the building. Elisa attached alligator clips to the electrodes in Frankie's neck.

Danny was leaning over the side, watching the string of lights. "Nothing happened," he said.

"So much for good intentions," said Howie.

"Not enough power," said Frankie. "We need Elisa in the circuit too." He took one of the clips from his own neck and attached it to Elisa's. "Now," he said, "we hold hands."

Suddenly, the bulbs in the string flared with a bright, Christmassy light. They spelled out WELCOME PARENTS. Below, the parents and children began to cheer and applaud with enthusiasm. By the light of the sign, Danny could see Ms. Cosgrove applauding and cheering right along with them.

"And those lights are in parallel," Frankie said, "not series. If one goes out, the rest of them stay on."

Danny knew that Parents' Night was a monster success!

MEL GILDEN is the author of the acclaimed *The Return of Captain Conquer,* published by Houghton Mifflin in 1986. His second novel, *Harry Newberry Says His Mom Is a Superhero,* will be published soon by Henry Holt and Company. Previous to these novels, Gilden had short stories published in such places as *Twilight Zone— The Magazine, The Magazine of Fantasy and Science Fiction,* and many original and reprint anthologies.

JOHN PIERARD is a freelance illustrator living in Manhattan. He is best known for his science fiction illustrations for *Isaac Asimov's Science Fiction Magazine, Distant Stars,* and SPI games such as Universe. He is co-illustrator of Time Machine #4: *Sail With Pirates* and Time Traveler #3: *The First Settlers,* and is illustrator of Time Machine #11: *Mission to World War II* and Time Machine #15: *Flame of the Inquisition.*

HOWLING GOOD FUN
FROM AVON CAMELOT

Meet the 5th graders of P.S. 13—
the craziest, creepiest kids ever!

M IS FOR MONSTER
    75423-1/$2.50 US/$3.25 CAN
by Mel Gilden; illustrated by John Pierard

BORN TO HOWL   75425-8/$2.50 US/$3.25 CAN
by Mel Gilden; illustrated by John Pierard

THERE'S A BATWING IN MY
    LUNCHBOX   75426-6/$2.75 US/$3.25 CAN
by Ann Hodgman; illustrated by John Pierard

THE PET OF FRANKENSTEIN
    75185-2/$2.50 US/$2.50 US/$3.25 CAN
by Mel Gilden; illustrated by John Pierard

Z IS FOR ZOMBIE 75686-2/$2.50 US/$3.25 CAN
by Mel Gilden; illustrated by John Pierard